"You Look Sensational,"

he said, his brown eyes devouring her twice—once in person, and again in the mirror.

Felicia stood immobile, shocked by how much she resembled her mother.

"What are you trying to do to me?" she demanded.

"Nothing," Roderick said reassuringly, "but take your picture, just as I said."

"You're trying to make me over. You're determined to revive my mother's image, and if I won't cooperate with you, you'll stoop to any trick to try to force me!"

"What are you afraid of, Felicia?" Roderick asked, his eyes darkening.

PATTI BECKMAN'S interesting locales and spirited characters will thoroughly delight her reading audience. She lives with her husband Charles, and their young daughter, along the Gulf Coast of Texas.

D1316711

Dear Reader:

Silhouette Books is pleased to announce the creation of a new line of contemporary romances—*Silhouette Special Editions*. Each month we'll bring you six new love stories written by the best of today's authors— Janet Dailey, Brooke Hastings, Laura Hardy, Sondra Stanford, Linda Shaw, Patti Beckman, and many others.

Silhouette Special Editions are written with American women in mind; they are for readers who want more: more story, more details and descriptions, more realism, and more *romance*. *Special Editions* are longer than most contemporary romances allowing for a closer look at the relationship between hero and heroine with emphasis on heightened romantic tension and greater sensuous and sensual detail. If you want more from a romance, be sure to look for *Silhouette Special Editions* on sale this February wherever you buy books.

We welcome any suggestions or comments, and I invite you to write us at the address below.

Karen Solem
Editor-in-Chief
Silhouette Books
P.O. Box 769
New York, N. Y. 10019

PATTI BECKMAN
Spotlight to Fame

Silhouette **Romance**

Published by Silhouette Books New York

America's Publisher of Contemporary Romance

Other Silhouette Books by Patti Beckman

Captive Heart
The Beachcomber
Louisiana Lady
Angry Lover
Love's Treacherous Journey

SILHOUETTE BOOKS, a Simon & Schuster Division of
GULF & WESTERN CORPORATION
1230 Avenue of the Americas, New York, N.Y. 10020

ISBN: 0-671-57124-9

First Silhouette Books printing January, 1982

10 9 8 7 6 5 4 3 2 1

America's Publisher of Contemporary Romance

Printed in the U.S.A.

To Jeanne—
Thank You

Chapter One

"Thank you for coming," Felicia Farr said to the class of assembled parents, who occupied the seats of their offspring. "It's always a pleasure to see such a good turnout for a PTA meeting. Your children have worked hard this year, and they are eager for you to see samples of their work. I hope you like our displays. Please make yourselves at home and feel free to ask me any questions you may have about your child's progress in this class."

With that, Felicia motioned for the parents to mingle with each other and view the notebooks, drawings, test papers and essays written by the students in her third-year Spanish class. She stood by her desk, her long blond hair knotted into a conservative chignon on the back of her head. A casual observer would have pronounced her attractive, but none of the parents in the room suspected the true extent of Felicia's beauty.

Her well-scrubbed face shone with a healthy glow, but the long, thick lashes that rimmed her eyes were blond, and thus, without mascara, they did little to define her deep blue eyes. And that was the way Felicia wanted it. She purposely chose plain clothes, sensible, stacked heels and a severe hairstyle. Maybe it was a form of rebellion against her childhood. But there was no way she could camouflage the erect carriage that she had learned as a young child from her mother. The aristocratic, haughty turn of her head, coupled with a subtle glance out of the corners of her eyes, gave her an unapproachable yet alluring quality that she didn't even know she possessed. It was a quality imitated by the girls in her class and eagerly discussed at length by the boys as they laid wagers about the extent and frequency of Felicia's love life and fantasized themselves the object of her affection.

But there was one person in the classroom that night who was not a parent, and he knew the possibilities that existed for the beauty and appeal of Felicia Farr.

Felicia's gaze flicked over the crowd of parents milling from desk to desk, flipping through notebooks and stopping to chat briefly with her about "Johnny" or "Susie's" work in her class that year. School was nearing a close, and Felicia had talked to some of the parents before, so she knew most of them. As usual, there was a core of parents who were always interested in what their children did. They supported the school and its programs. They were the parents who attended PTA meetings and came for conferences during the year. It was the parents of the children who were failing who never showed up. They were the people Felicia yearned to talk to. But they never came to any school functions. What a pity, Felicia thought. No wonder their children did so poorly in school, with no support at home for their efforts.

In the mixed assemblage of Hispanic, Indian and

European heritage parents that made up the population of most of New Mexico, Felicia's blue eyes settled on the face of a man who stood across the room from her. Unlike the other parents, he did not browse among the displays. Instead, he stood leaning against the green plaster wall, his arms folded across his chest, his large brown eyes trained on her.

Lightning coursed through Felicia's veins as she met his gaze and realized that he had been staring at her. It was an unsettling experience, reacting like that to a student's father. A pink color tinged her cheeks as she realized such feelings were usually reserved for cocktail parties, where the chemistry of the evening, combined with the alchemy of alcoholic beverages, caused people to drop their defenses and respond emotionally to total strangers. Never before had she felt so drawn to a man at first sight. And yet, there was something familiar about him—something about his thick black hair, the high cheekbones, the strong jaw and nose, and the dark skin that made her recoil from his stare. Did he have a son in her class who had given her a lot of trouble? Was she reacting to the emotional image this man conjured up in her mind because of his resemblance to his son?

Who is he? she wondered. She had never seen him before, she was positive, but there was something so powerful and strong in his presence that she felt she almost knew this man. Why did parents wait until the last PTA meeting of the year to come to discuss their children's problems? she grumbled silently to herself. How much good would it do to even talk to him, now that the year was almost over?

Felicia sighed and decided she was going to have to make the first move. The man just stood there, shamelessly devouring her with his eyes. She could no longer stand being the object of his scrutiny. She stepped from behind her desk and made a move toward him, but a student's father stopped her.

"Miss Farr, Felipe thinks you are the greatest teacher he has ever had," Mr. Sanchez said, stepping into Felicia's path. "Are you going to teach fourth-year Spanish next year?"

"I don't know, Mr. Sanchez," Felicia said. "Our assignments haven't been finalized yet. But I can tell you that Felipe will do well, no matter who his teacher is. He's a fine student. I was lucky to have him in my class."

Mr. Sanchez smiled broadly, and Felicia walked past him, only to feel her heart pound as her gaze once again turned toward the spot in the back of the room where the dark, suave-looking man had stood. Suddenly she felt a quick stab of disappointment. The spot was empty. The man had disappeared.

Felicia looked quickly around the room. She caught a glimpse of a tall, dark man leaving through the doorway into the hall. She hurried to catch up with him, but when she reached the doorway, he was gone. She looked down the corridor. The overhead lights gleamed on the polished hardwood floors. There was no echo of footsteps, no trace of the man. He had simply vanished. How strange! she thought.

The remainder of the evening Felicia went through the motions of talking to parents, and discussing her goals for the class and how they had been met. But she spoke automatically; her mind was somewhere else completely. The mental image of a dark, foreboding man kept intruding, unwanted, into her thoughts. And try as she might, she could not erase it.

The next week found Felicia making a futile search for the identity of the man who had invaded her classroom and her thoughts. But no student claimed him as a parent, and the principal had sent no one to observe her during the PTA meeting. Had he ambled into her room by mistake? she wondered. That was the only logical conclusion. But why had he stared at her in that strange, penetrating fashion?

Another thing that puzzled Felicia was her reluctance to discuss the incident with Don Hamilton. They had a relaxed, easy relationship, and she usually told him her feelings about things. As a matter of fact, she had confided in him her feelings about her mother, a deep secret she had kept locked in her heart since childhood. So why should she guard her reaction to a strange man who had walked into her class by mistake and had spent a few innocent moments staring at her?

"Innocent," Felicia mumbled to herself. That was the key to the whole thing. It had not been so innocent. There had been a knowing, threatening glint in the strange man's eyes when he had stared at her, and Felicia had responded to his visual embrace with a pleasure she didn't dare admit to herself. He had liked something about the way she looked, and she had enjoyed being looked at in that manner in spite of the fact that she had vowed never to get through life by using her appearance.

Fortunately, the last weeks of school took on a hectic, frantic tone that stripped Felicia of the time to think about the strange man, and she put him out of her mind. She and Don were the senior-class sponsors, and they had a long list of last-minute details to attend to before the seniors could roll off on buses for their senior trip. Don was the high school coach.

"These kids really tried," she said to Don one morning in the teachers' lounge, "but they just couldn't raise the kind of money needed to make a trip to the Coast."

Don sat across from Felicia at a long table. In spite of the warm, dry weather, he held a cup of hot coffee in one hand. His sandy-colored, curly hair, blue eyes and clean-cut features gave him a healthy, youthful look that appealed to Felicia. Sometimes Don got lost in a group of rowdy high school boys on the baseball field, blending in with them because he looked so young. Felicia had a soft spot in her heart for her students, and Don was so much a part of the school scene that she felt comfortable and relaxed with him.

Felicia spread out a map of the United States on the table. "We're just going to have to go someplace closer to home," Felicia said. "Do you think the kids will be terribly disappointed?"

"A little," Don said, his blue eyes staring into the cup in his hand. Then he looked at her. "But they know how things are financially. They must realize the trip to the Coast is out. Just how much money do they have in the senior-class treasury?"

"Not very much, with prices as they are," Felicia said. "If we spend the night out on the road, we'll have to go somewhere within the state. We could go farther if we didn't have to pay motel bills, but I hardly think we could organize a camping trip at this late date. Imagine the problems trying to get food ready, making sure everyone has sleeping gear, et cetera."

"Let me look at the map," Don said, turning the large, colored paper around so he could see New Mexico easily. He studied it a minute, put his coffee cup aside and ran his finger over the drawing of the state.

"Well, the most logical place is Carlsbad Caverns, of course," he said.

"But the class already voted not to go there," Felicia said.

"Only because they thought the Coast would be more glamorous. Most people don't know what's sitting in their own backyard because they take it for granted. There are lots of tourists who have more information about Carlsbad than the natives because the tourists made a special trip to see the place. Just because it's close to them, Carlsbad doesn't seem quite exotic enough to most kids to justify spending their trip money to see it. But I bet most of them have never been there, and it's really a spectacular place."

"I hope you don't expect me to be the one to try to foist Carlsbad off on them," Felicia said, her face registering dismay.

"Let me handle it," Don said.

That afternoon, Don called a meeting of the senior class to announce that their treasury lacked enough money for them to take a senior trip. The groans could be heard on the second floor of the two-story, adobe schoolhouse. Then, as if he had had a sudden inspiration, Don diverted the class's despair into a glimmer of hope when he said there was a possibility, just a slight possibility, that they could afford maybe a two-day trip, if they didn't have outlandish expectations.

When Don called for a show of hands for how many students had visited Carlsbad, only three hands went up. And a grateful senior class, marveling at the cleverness of its male senior sponsor, eagerly signed up for the trip.

"That was very slick," Felicia teased later, "the way you conned those kids."

"It wasn't a con," Don said defensively, but with a grin on his lips. "I was just using a quirk of human nature to my advantage. It's called the law of lowering expectations. Let the kids think they can't have anything, and they'll gladly settle for anything they can get. They lowered their expectations from a trip to the Coast because they thought a trip of any kind was out of the question."

"No wonder you get along so well with the boys." Felicia laughed. "You've got them right in the palm of your hand!" Don was well liked and respected among the male members of the student body, but the girls were another matter. For them, Don represented the ultimate in high school machismo. While most girls longed for a date with the captain of the football team, the girls at San Pedro High vied shamelessly for the attentions of one very appealing baseball coach and math teacher. The jealousy Don created among the girls made it difficult for him to supervise them as casually as he did the boys.

Two weeks later, a large yellow school bus, lettered proudly with CARLSBAD OR BUST, pulled out from the high school campus and rolled south to Whites City, the town at the entrance to the cave. Felicia sat in the front seat, flanked by exuberant seniors tasting the deliciousness of freedom from parental restrictions for the next two days. Don drove, and they both joined in the endless rounds of high school cheers and traditional school songs that speeded them along the way.

"Now remember," Don announced to the assembled group as they approached the entrance to the cave, "Stala*ctites* hang from the ceiling and stala*gmites* rise up from the floor. And that is all the educational information you are going to get from me on this trip," he said with a chuckle. "I'm on vacation, too. Everyone have a good time, and we'll meet back at the entrance to the caves to see the bats fly out at sunset."

With that, eager seniors scattered in all directions. Some headed directly into the mouth of the cave while others made their way up the steep trail back to the headquarters building to browse in the souvenir sections of the gift shop before taking their tour.

The steep mile-and-three-quarters trip down the trail didn't particularly appeal to Felicia, so she opted for the elevator ride down, leaving Don at the gaping entrance to the mammoth cavern. The elevator transported her 830 feet below the surface of the ground in a matter of moments. She stepped out into a damp, dimly lit underground cavern that had been discovered in 1901 by James White. The cool fifty-six-degree temperature made her shiver momentarily as she was almost overcome by the oppressive dampness in the air. The sensation stirred nostalgic feelings for the coast of Spain, where she had spent most of the last thirteen years. She had adjusted only gradually to the dry, hot climate of New Mexico during the last year that she had been back in the States.

Felicia was adjusting the light sweater she had brought to protect her from the chill when she felt a presence behind her that penetrated through her distraction with the sweater. For some reason she felt reluctant to turn around, as if she knew she would not like what she would see. So she walked toward the bright yellow snack bar, which looked ridiculously out of place in the primitive confines of a huge, beige cavern deep beneath the earth.

Just then, she heard a "click," which captured her attention in spite of herself, and she turned abruptly to see a camera pointed at her. The hand that held it was dark, and the face it partly concealed was smiling a strange, arrogant grin that unnerved Felicia. The camera clicked again, and a light blinded her.

Before Felicia could protest at having her photograph taken without her permission, the man pushed through the doors to the elevators, hopped on one and was whisked out of sight. Felicia ran after him, but she was too late. The sign read ELEVATOR EVERY FIVE MINUTES, so she was trapped beneath the surface of the ground until the mechanical monster decided it was time to make its swift descent and pick up another load of tourists.

"Who *is* he?" she muttered to herself, her voice

15

echoing slightly off the walls of the small, empty room. "First my classroom and now here. It couldn't be just a coincidence. There's something spooky about this whole thing, and I've got to find out what it is."

Felicia paced nervously in front of the elevator doors. When she reached the surface a few minutes later, as she expected, the strange man she pursued was nowhere to be found. In the off-season during May, the visitors to Carlsbad were few, so it was not difficult to check the snack bar, the gift shop, the main lobby and the grounds outside the building.

Felicia stood looking over the mountains surrounding the cavern, her eyes squinting against the bright sun, her brain a torrent of troubled thoughts. Was she in some kind of danger from this strange man who had intruded into her life uninvited? Maybe the time had come to tell Don about him. There didn't seem much that Don could do, but he was a clever sort of fellow. At least if anything happened to her, someone should know about the strange man and report his behavior to the police. It certainly was suspicious, to say the least.

For the remainder of the day, Felicia couldn't keep her mind on what she was doing. She had decided to wait until they were back at the motel and the kids bedded down before telling Don about her fears. There was no point in spoiling his day. But all afternoon, as she and Don toured the various caverns together, she neither heard nor saw what was said. Her gaze searched the other visitors for a glimpse of a tall, dark man with a strong jaw and nose. A man who both fascinated, repelled and frightened her. A man who had stirred in her a vortex of emotions she had never before experienced.

As planned, the class met outside the cavern entrance just before sunset. Don counted heads, and Felicia called names just to be sure no one had been forgotten. Confident that the entire class had arrived, Don led them to the benches built in a semicircle around the cavern entrance. A ranger stood at the foot of the small outdoor auditorium. Felicia was about to escort the last girl to her seat to hear the lecture on the Mexican bats as they flew out of the cave in hordes of hundreds of thousands, when she felt a warm hand on her elbow. A tingle raced up her arm and made her heart race, leaving her breathless. She didn't have to turn around. She knew instinctively who it was.

"Y-you, again!" she choked. "Who are you, and what do you want?"

The strange man let go of her arm, and for an instant, he stared at her with his large brown eyes caressing her face.

Felicia gasped and stepped back. But she felt hypnotized by the brown eyes that, up close, she could see were sparkled with green flecks that caught the rays of the dying sun and shot them at her with a glitter of amusement combined with something resembling deep concern.

Felicia stood motionless, just back of the last row of students, who were unaware of what was going on. Then she felt a shock as she saw the strange man turn and stride away from her up the steps. She couldn't let him get away from her this time. She had to know who he was and what he wanted! She ran after him and grabbed him by the arm just before he disappeared between a motor home and a large van.

"Wait!" she demanded, pulling on his sleeve. "You have no right to . . . to . . ." To do what? she wondered vaguely.

The man stopped, turned and looked down at her. Suddenly she felt very vulnerable and afraid. Maybe he had tricked her into following her here, sandwiched between two large vehicles. He was much stronger than she was. He could easily force her into either of the vehicles with him. Was he a deranged lunatic who had chosen her for his next victim?

Felicia's entire body prickled with fear. A warm, dry breeze swept across her skin, and she was acutely aware of the press of her clothes on her body. Apprehension heightened all her senses at once.

"Never mind," Felicia managed to say, her head pounding hard from fright, her knees quaking.

"It's all right," he said, his voice calm and low. "I'm not here to harm you in any way." His tone showed he had read the fear in her eyes. "I just wanted to see you again."

"What for?" she asked suspiciously, backing away a step.

"To give you this," he said huskily, and his hand reached out, encircled her wrist and pulled her to him. His dark face lowered to hers, and he tilted up her unwilling chin with a firm pull she couldn't resist. His warm lips found hers, and again a lightning bolt of fear shot through her as she felt herself lose control of her freedom. Strong arms encircled her back and waist, and hot breaths swept across her cheek as the strange man pulled her tighter and tighter in his arms.

Felicia struggled at first, trying to push back against the hard muscles of the strange man's chest, but they were like iron bands. She tried biting him, but his strong mouth kept hers its prisoner. She even kicked him in the shins, but he stood motionless, as if he hadn't felt the blows from her walking shoes. Then, exhausted, Felicia gave up the battle, partly because she had no strength left to fight, and partly because she began to enjoy the closeness of this man and the feel of his powerful arms enveloping her in their cocoon. In spite of her fear, she began to melt against this man who had entered her life against her will and who seemed determined to turn her emotions upside down.

Then, before she realized he had released her, the man had withdrawn from the embrace, and he strode away quickly. Felicia stood there dumbfounded, unable to gather her scattered thoughts, unable to figure out what to do.

Chapter Two

Felicia waited anxiously in the doctor's outer office. Her emotions were mixed, her thoughts troubled.

When she had returned from the trip to Carlsbad, she had found herself so puzzled over the behavior of the strange man who had invaded her life that she had drifted through the closing ritual of school in something of a fog.

But once school was actually over and Don had departed for summer courses at college, Felicia again experienced the gnawing hunger that dominated her life—to meet face to face with her mother. Surely this summer would be different. A miracle would take place, and she would crack through the fortress walls her mother had built around her life. But all of Felicia's letters remained unanswered.

She could no longer bear the uncertainty, the waiting

for an invitation that never came. Finally, she became determined to take aggressive action. She searched her memory and came up with the name of a family doctor who had treated her mother years ago. She phoned and was delighted to find that old Dr. Ambrewster was still treating her mother. Felicia explained briefly the problem she was having trying to communicate with her mother. "I think it would be better for us to discuss this in my office," the doctor had said. And his nurse had then arranged for an appointment.

Now, when she was ushered into Dr. Ambrewster's office, Felicia felt the strain she was under. She was filled with apprehension and uncertainty. She took a deep breath and sat in a chair before the doctor's desk. How could she find the words to explain the emotional hunger she felt to find her mother and the frustration and bitterness at having all doors slammed in her face? She took some reassurance from the fact that Dr. Ambrewster was a silver-haired man with a kind, fatherly manner.

"I—I don't know if you're aware of the situation between my mother and me, Dr. Ambrewster," Felicia began. "She sent me off to boarding school in Spain when I was ten years old. She visited me a few times, then stopped seeing me altogether. I came back to the States hoping to make some contact with her. She refuses to see me. She won't answer my letters." Felicia looked at the doctor with tear-filled eyes. "Can you tell me why she hates me so? What did I ever do to her to make her abandon me like that?"

Dr. Ambrewster frowned, returning Felicia's tear-filled gaze with a look of compassion. "Yes, I'm aware of the situation between you and your mother, Miss Farr. I can assure you that your mother doesn't hate you. To the contrary, she loves you very much. . . ."

"I can't believe that!" Felicia cried bitterly. "How

21

could she ship me off to Spain like that if she really loved me?"

The doctor sighed. "Sometimes life forces people to make decisions that break their hearts. I'll never believe your mother sent you to Spain without a great sense of loss."

"But she did it!" Felicia retorted. "America's most famous model didn't want a teen-age daughter around to remind her and her public of how old she really was."

"I can understand how you feel." Dr. Ambrewster nodded sympathetically. "You have a right to be bitter. But I believe your mother was never a strong-willed woman. Your stepfather had a strange influence over her. He was an ambitious man. He managed all her affairs. He felt you would be a hindrance to your mother's career. He convinced your mother to send you to a boarding school."

"But she could have visited me more often!" Felicia protested. "I can count on one hand the times she stopped off on a flight through Spain. A day here, a day there. A lot of lavish presents to make up for not being with me on Christmas and my birthdays.

"Now that my mother is no longer in the spotlight of fame, you'd think she'd be willing to see me, to let me get to know her a little to make up for missing out on knowing her when I was a child."

Suddenly a flood of tears spilled forth. The agony of her lonely childhood was so indelibly engraved on her consciousness, she could no longer pretend it didn't matter. In a voice choked with emotion she cried, "I came back to the States to find a part of my childhood I never had. I'll never feel whole or completely adult until I've resolved those feelings of deprivation. And the only way I can do that is to get to know my mother. I'm love-starved, Dr. Ambrewster, for affection and attention from my mother. I know that sounds ridiculous coming from a twenty-three-year-old woman, but it's the truth."

She felt a gentle hand on her shoulder and felt a tissue thrust into her palm.

"Felicia," Dr. Ambrewster said, "your mother's had a nervous breakdown. Right now she's in no condition to see anyone. I think her guilt has been the final blow—guilt because she treated you so miserably. After your stepfather died, she asked me what I thought about bringing you back to the States. I urged her to do it. But by then she was so ashamed of what she had done to you, she no longer had the courage to face you."

"So first it was fear of ruining her career, and then it was guilt that kept us apart," Felicia said stonily. "And what was her excuse when I came back here? I made it clear that I wanted to see her, but she refused without even saying why!"

"I'm afraid I can't explain it, Felicia. As I told you, I'm not a psychiatrist. She isn't even seeing her close friends. All I can tell you is that she had a nervous breakdown. Perhaps she has had so many guilty feelings over the years that she can't believe you would forgive her."

"It's not a matter of forgiving her," Felicia said, her voice still shaking but under better control now. "It's something I must do for my own sake, for my own peace of mind. I need to know something about the kind of person I came from. Can you understand that, Dr. Ambrewster? I don't think anyone who has grown up in normal circumstances can grasp the significance of the psychological need I have. It's almost like the adopted child who feels compelled to search for his biological parents, to find out who and what they were. I have all kinds of fancy pictures of my mother, stories by the score in gossip and glamour magazines about Francine Farr. But they don't tell me who my mother really is."

"Of course they don't," Dr. Ambrewster agreed.

"How . . . how sick is my mother now? Is she in any danger?"

"One can never be certain in a case of emotional depression. I have been treating her for a heart condition for a number of years. But her immediate health problem, as I say, is emotional. I think the years of dieting; of trying to please her public, her employers and your stepfather; of working long hours past the point of exhaustion has broken her health, physically and emotionally. And added to that is the terrible burden of guilt over the way she treated you. She has suffered a great deal."

"So have I!" Felicia said.

"True, but your health is good. Be patient, Felicia. As soon as she's under the care of a good psychiatrist, he can make a judgment about her condition. I'm sure he'll let you see her as soon as he thinks it's feasible."

"Don't count on it," Felicia sighed. "I imagine my mother can pretty well get her way under any circumstances. By virtue of the fact that she's the once-famous Francine Farr, she'll have the psychiatrist eating out of her hand in no time. And if she decides she still doesn't want to see me, no amount of pleading on my part will change that."

"Well, of course any doctor will act in the best interest of the patient. You have to understand that. But I know your mother well enough to assure you that she will come around. She wants to get to know you, too, Felicia. She's just scared."

Felicia nodded silently.

"Now, about her medical problem," the doctor continued. "She needs to be in a private sanitarium under the care of a good psychiatrist. She may need electroshock therapy. That kind of treatment can be quite expensive. She doesn't have any money—not even health insurance. She's broke."

"Broke!" Felicia exclaimed incredulously. "But she was worth a fortune. . . ."

"Yes, at one time she was. Unfortunately, your stepfather managed to spend most of it. He made some poor investments that just about wiped them out by the time he died. The last few years, your mother has been living very frugally. The kind of specialized care she needs does not come cheap. Six months of treatment could cost as much as you earn in an entire year as a schoolteacher."

Felicia was stunned. Where could she possibly get that kind of money? "A whole year's salary?" she choked.

"That's right. Do you have any money saved?"

"No. I just barely managed to scrape together enough for fare back to the States. I've spent this year's salary on a few clothes and some furniture—plus living expenses."

"Well." Dr. Ambrewster shook his head solemnly. "There's always the state hospital. They are under-staffed and can't give patients the concentrated therapy your mother needs. It will take a long time, but if there's no other choice . . ."

"No!" Felicia heard herself blurt out. "Don't do that. I don't want her to go to the state hospital. I'll raise the money somehow."

"Good girl," Dr. Ambrewster said with a smile, and Felicia realized the full potency of her mother's image. Dr. Ambrewster didn't care what kind of hardship Felicia had to undergo to raise the money her mother needed for proper care. All he was concerned about was that Francine Farr should have the best. Her mother's magic, golden image was almost as powerful as ever. And why not? She had been the reigning model of glamour, a personality and a face and body that had captured the hearts of fans all across the country.

Only now did Felicia understand why the money from her mother had dwindled so the last few years. When she had first gone to Spain she had been the best-dressed girl at the most exclusive boarding school. But the schools became less and less prestigious. She had barely managed to make it through college. It wasn't until this moment that she realized how much her mother had sacrificed to keep those final checks coming. Had her mother felt obliged to send money the last few years when she was struggling to put food on her own table because of a sense of guilt and obligation? Or was it possible that her mother remembered the blue-eyed little girl who had been sent away at the age of ten, and she still loved the daughter she had sent to Spain?

With Don off at a university for the summer, Felicia had no one to advise her about how to get a loan. She had been back in the States only a year, so she was still learning the intricacies of American business. First, she went to the teachers' credit union, where she was promptly turned down. She had no collateral, and the sum she needed was much too large for a simple signature loan. Three banks only laughed at her request, citing her lack of collateral and any kind of credit rating. Two loan-company officers were sympathetic but sent her packing within five minutes.

Tired and discouraged, Felicia sat in her simple apartment at the end of a long day filled with rejections. She was overcome with despair. With no money to get her mother proper care, she might not get to see her for years—maybe never. A gnawing need to know her mother had been growing in her for a long time, and when she had boarded the transatlantic flight for the United States, she had felt sure that the end of her yearning was in sight. But ever since arriving, she had run into one obstacle after another. And here it was, a full year since her return, and her goal seemed more remote than ever.

Felicia walked into the pullman kitchen of her efficiency apartment. Although it was past suppertime, she found her appetite had died along with her chances of obtaining a loan. She opened the refrigerator mechanically and took out a bottle of diet soft drink. While she had no problem with her weight, she had never cared for the syrupy taste of sugared drinks. In fact, she was something of a health food nut, the one luxury she allowed herself. She took vitamins regularly, ate small, simple meals of mostly raw fruits and vegetables, and made sure she got enough protein by eating yogurt and nuts. The few treats she allowed herself came from health food stores and were expensive, but she did not splurge in any other way.

Instead of going into debt for her furniture, Felicia had located a store that leased furniture with an option to buy. She had selected a light blue hide-a-bed for her apartment, a matching chair, an end table with a lamp, and one bookcase for her books of classical Spanish literature. On a beginning teacher's salary, there had not been anything left over for wall hangings and the other little knickknacks that turn a sterile apartment into a comfortable haven from the world. She still had a year of payments on the used car she had bought. In the spread-out topography of the United States, with its lack of reliable public transportation, Felicia had found her car a necessity.

So here she was, one year after coming back to the United States, still no closer to getting to know her mother than when she first arrived. Little did Felicia dream that the hand of fate was, at this moment, poised at her front door, ready to knock. Literally!

At first, Felicia ignored the raps at the apartment door. She was in no mood to talk to anyone. Maybe they would think she wasn't home and would go away. But the repeated knocking convinced her that a persistent soul on the other side of the door would not take no for an answer. Probably some salesman working the last shift who had seen her come in and wouldn't be put off, she grumbled under her breath.

Felicia opened the door and gasped. Blocking the doorway with his large, well-built frame was the mysterious, dark-complected stranger! He had been in her thoughts almost constantly since the school trip to Carlsbad; but today, for the first time, she had put him out of her mind because of more pressing considerations. It was as if he sensed she had dropped him to second place on her list of mental priorities and had come to claim his rightful place at the top.

"You!" she choked. "How did you find me? Who are you, and what do you want?"

"May I come in?" he asked, his brown eyes roving over her entire frame.

Felicia stood frozen. She didn't know whether to slam the door in his face, scream, or make a dash for the phone to call the police.

"I . . . I don't know," she hesitated, looking past him to see if there was anyone outside that could come to her aid if she should scream. The street was deserted.

"I'm not going to hurt you," he said, his voice so convincing that Felicia didn't believe him for a minute. He was too suave, too sure of himself, too polite, she concluded. She started to slam the door shut, but he wedged his powerful shoulders between the door and the jamb, and stood firm.

"Listen one minute before you kick me out," he said smoothly. "If I wanted to harm you, I had my chance at Carlsbad. You were all alone with me out in the parking lot. A simple kiss was all I took, and I assure you it won't happen again. I just want to talk to you."

Felicia trained her blue eyes on the strange man's face. Try as she might, she couldn't read the intent in his expression. The dark eyes, hair and skin gave him a foreboding appearance, but the strength of his argument rang true. Besides, she wanted to find out who he was and what he wanted. The final point in his favor was the obvious fact that if he was determined to enter her apartment, there really wasn't a great deal she could do to stop him, seeing that he was halfway in already.

Silently and slowly, Felicia released her pressure against the door. Warily, she stepped back into the apartment, keeping her eyes trained on the strange man.

"Thank you," he said with a large grin. "That's more like it." He straightened his suit coat and transferred a large manila envelope from one hand to the other in the process.

Suddenly Felicia felt her cheeks sting with embarrassment as she recalled the kiss the stranger had "taken" from her, as he had put it. Did he realize that she had actually enjoyed the feel of his mouth on hers, the close warmth of his body as he pressed her tightly to him? She recalled with shame the pleasure he had stirred up in her, and she diverted her eyes.

"Felicia," he began.

"You know my name?" she spluttered.

"But of course," he said, as if it were the most natural thing in the world that he should know her name. "That's why I'm here."

"I'm afraid I don't understand," she said.

"Of course you don't," he agreed with a smile. "May we sit down so I can explain?"

Felicia still harbored a suspicion that the strange man had come on a mission dictated by a deranged mind, but her curiosity was beginning to get the better of her, so she reluctantly agreed.

When she was seated on the hide-a-bed made up into its daytime function as a sofa, she motioned for him to sit in the matching blue chair which faced her. For a long moment the man's brown eyes flicked over Felicia, stopping here and there to linger on her face and the curve of her hips under the clinging, green knit fabric of her shirtwaist dress. Then his gaze slid down her lanky legs, which she had crossed.

At the same time, Felicia studied this strange man who had forced his way into her life, and she had to admit that she was not entirely turned off by his looks. There was something disturbing about him, but she couldn't attribute it to the thick black hair, the large brown eyes with green flecks, or the high cheekbones balanced by a strong jaw and nose. He certainly had a physique designed to make any young woman's heart jump, and his light green suit was in impeccable style. What was it about him that gave her that nervous, churning feeling?

"Well?" Felicia said at last. "You said you wanted to talk to me."

"Yes," he said, placing the manila envelope on the end table near him. "But first, I must apologize about the incident at Carlsbad. It was just a whim. I should have realized it could give you the impression that I'm some sort of fiend."

Felicia moved uneasily on the couch, wondering how she could have been so stupid as to let this strange man into her apartment. Just what was he leading up to, anyway?

"I have a proposition . . . no, that's a bad choice of

words," he corrected himself. "I have an offer to make you."

"An offer?" Felicia asked guardedly.

"I've been looking for you a long time, Felicia Farr," the man said with a degree of emotion that surprised her.

"What for?" she asked, clasping her hands in her lap nervously and picking at the cuticle of one nail.

"Because of these," he said, handing Felicia the envelope he had brought in with him.

Felicia hesitated. Her eyes met his above the flat expanse of manila paper closing the gap between them, and for an instant she was back at Carlsbad, her lips stinging from a strange man's kiss as he strode off, leaving her bewildered and shocked at her response to him.

Gingerly, Felicia accepted the envelope. She turned the envelope over and unfastened the metal clasp. She reached in, and her hand touched stiff paper. All at once, all the movies she had ever seen in Spain about blackmail flashed into her mind as she realized she was holding a stack of photographs. Had this man come here to blackmail her? But what about? She had certainly lead a circumspect life in Spain, chaperoned as she was at all times. And on her return to the States, she had only gradually felt herself melting into the American way of dating, so she had nothing in her background, distant or recent, that anyone could use for blackmail. Besides, she didn't have any money, anyway.

Felicia slid the photographs out slowly, almost afraid to look at them. She had a strange premonition that this tableau—her sitting on her sofa, photographs in hand, with a stranger leaning in her direction from his chair opposite her—would come back to haunt her as an act which would somehow change her life forever.

When she had taken the photographs completely out

of the envelope, Felicia sat motionless for a moment with the pictures face down. She stared at the flat white paper and wondered if she dare look at the other side.

"Go ahead, look at them," the man urged.

With growing apprehension, Felicia turned the photographs over. She was totally unprepared for the image that met her gaze.

"Why, these are photographs of my mother!" she exclaimed.

"Yes. Francine Farr, the most photographed model in the history of advertising. That is, until now."

Felicia thumbed through the stack of pictures. Her mother smiled coyly from the glossy paper, her wide smile and straight, white teeth a tribute to the cult of beauty that she had launched early in her career. The long, platinum hair, the deep blue eyes fringed with heavy lashes, and the chiseled nose situated in a perfectly oval face had made Francine Farr one of the most famous beauties in the world. Her lovely features had been a familiar sight on billboards, in slick magazines and on national TV programs in the U.S. and abroad. Most of her career had been identified with the Magic Glo Cosmetics line that she had made famous. For years, until her beauty began to fade, she had been the Magic Glo woman, a symbol and a promise to countless other women all over the world who wanted to be beautiful.

Felicia put the pictures aside. "Mr.—?"

"Bearstern," the man replied.

"Bearstern?"

"Yes. Roderick Bearstern. My last name is Indian."

"Oh," she said, understanding now the man's dark coloring and high cheekbones. Then she frowned, repeating the unusual name slowly. "Bearstern. . . . that's familiar. . . ." Suddenly she gasped. "Of course! John Bearstern was president of the Magic Glo Cosmetics line when my mother was a model!"

The man before her nodded. "Yes—my father. He started the line. Made a fortune with it. . . ."

"You mean my mother made a fortune *for* him," Felicia said coldly, with a rush of angry passion that brought color to her cheeks. "It was your father and my stepfather who used and drove my mother, demanding more and more of her for the sake of the product. They destroyed her health and robbed me of a mother for most of my childhood!"

Roderick Bearstern seemed taken by surprise by her outburst. Finally he said, "I can't answer for the policy of my father or the company. I haven't been in the business that long."

"You have taken over your father's business?"

"In a sense. I'm chairman of the board of a large holding company, a conglomerate that owns several businesses. One of them is the Magic Glo Cosmetics line. My father retired a few years ago."

Felicia thought that it was irrational to direct her hatred of his father to the man before her. But she had hated the name Bearstern for so many years, it was difficult to be reasonable about it. Those years she was growing up in Spain, she had been bitter toward her mother, but she had hated her stepfather and John Bearstern. Doctor Ambrewster had only confirmed what she had suspected all along—that her mother had been weak, easily swayed by her husband and the man who also controlled her life, John Bearstern. They had persuaded Francine Farr to ship her daughter off to a school in Spain.

"Why have you come here? What do you want, Mr. Bearstern?" she asked coldly. "You walked into my classroom uninvited, cornered me at Carlsbad Caverns and took my picture, and now you bring me photographs of my mother. Don't you think it's time you explained what all of this means?" Her voice was sharp with exasperation.

He made an openhanded gesture. "I want to revive the image of your mother," he said simply.

"What do you mean, revive her image?" Felicia demanded. "You mean reprint these old photographs?"

"No. Not at all. I want to give the public another opportunity to worship the beauty and magic of Francine Farr, and I want to do it through you."

Felicia looked at him incredulously. "Mr. Bearstern, you're not making a great deal of sense."

"Felicia," he said patiently, "do you have any idea how much you are the image of your mother? You have the same proud, almost haughty, turn of head; the same erect, aristocratic carriage; and that feigned look of innocence that drives men wild. I want to re-create the Francine Farr image by using *you.* Imagine the promotion, the buildup. Francine Farr's own daughter, a fresh young replica of her famous mother, once again the beautiful symbol for Magic Glo Cosmetics."

Felicia's eyes grew wide in disbelief. The man was insane! The last thing she had ever considered being was a model. She had her mother's modeling career to blame for her lonely, bitter childhood. How she despised the profession that had robbed her of a mother in the years she had needed her the most!

"Mr. Bearstern, you're wasting your time," she snapped. "I can assure you that the last thing I would ever consider is a modeling career. I saw firsthand what it did to my mother. It turned her into a slave to her own beauty. She had no time for a normal life, a family—" Her voice was dangerously close to breaking. "Find somebody else to sell your cosmetics!"

"But it doesn't have to be that way," he protested. "Perhaps my father *was* to blame for demanding so much of your mother. Maybe she *did* give up too much. I wouldn't ask that of you. . . ."

"You'll never convince me of that," Felicia said bitterly.

"Give me a chance," Bearstern said.

"Never!" Felicia said icily. "I think it's time you left, sir. I have nothing further to discuss with you."

"You don't know what you're turning down," Bearstern argued. "I'm prepared to offer you a contract for ten times as much money as you're making teaching school. And that's just for starters."

Angrily, Felicia stood up, spilling the photographs to the floor. "I know exactly what I'm turning down!" she retorted. "Right now, my mother needs hospital care way beyond my ability to pay," Felicia blurted out. "If you were offering me a job doing anything else, I'd jump at the chance to make that kind of money. But nothing in this world could induce me to get into modeling. It's a profane way to make a living. It robs a woman of every shred of human decency. I saw it happen to my mother, and by God, it's not going to happen to me!"

Felicia's blue eyes blazed with a fury that left her shaking and cold. Her lanky legs wobbled as she sought to support herself in her indignation and wrath.

Slowly, Bearstern picked up the photographs from the floor. His brown eyes met her blue ones, and she saw in them a glint that unnerved her. "Think it over," he said, pressing the pictures in her hands.

"There's nothing to think over," she said tartly, snatching her hands back.

"I'm not giving up, Felicia," Bearstern said. "Once I have my mind made up, I never give up. I'm used to getting what I want, and I want *you*. You'll change your mind. Mark my words."

"You can't threaten me," Felicia warned.

"It's not a threat, Felicia. It's a promise." With that, Roderick Bearstern strode to the apartment door. His large frame blocked the entryway as he turned for one last comment. "You'll be mine, Felicia Farr, and sooner than you think."

Chapter Three

"Miss Farr?" the masculine, familiar voice on the other end of the telephone line asked.

"Yes," Felicia answered, sifting through a series of voices stored in her mind, trying to recall who possessed this one.

"This is Mr. Humbolt."

"Oh, yes." Felicia smiled. Now the voice suddenly took on a face and a personality. It was the principal from her high school.

"I've had a call that may interest you. A firm called me this morning looking for someone who speaks Castilian Spanish. They have summer employment for someone with your qualifications."

"They called you?" Felicia asked, a little surprised.

"Yes. It seems the secretary concluded that a high school would have a Spanish teacher, and they might just find one who had been in Spain long enough to pick up the dialect there. When I told them your background, they were delighted."

"Did you give them my name?" Felicia asked, excitement beginning to bubble up in her.

"No. I told them I'd contact you myself first to see if you were interested. They want you to travel to Spain to do some interpreting for a salesman. Something about farm machinery, I believe the secretary said."

"Why, yes, Mr. Humbolt, I'd be interested," Felicia said, her blue eyes sparkling.

Quickly, she took down the necessary information.

Ever since her discouraging rounds to various lending institutions, which had rejected her applications for a loan, Felicia had been sunk in despair.

A summer job had seemed an answer to her dilemma. Her teacher's salary was spread over a twelve-month pay period, so her living expenses for the summer were covered. Any money she earned from a summer job could be spent on her mother's medical expenses.

She had searched want ads in the newspaper, sent off letters of application and had even placed her own ad in the classified section of the newspaper, listing her qualifications and offering her services for the summer. She had applied at the state employment commission and registered at private employment agencies. So far, her efforts at finding a summer job had ended in frustration. Nothing was available.

Now, out of the blue, had come what might be the answer to her problem.

Clutching the address she had scribbled on a piece of paper, Felicia twirled around the room, her blond hair flying out behind her. "Yipee," she squealed. "Maybe this is the answer to my prayers."

Trying to bridle her excitement, she focused her blue eyes on the phone number Mr. Humbolt had given her and dialed with shaking fingers.

"Lakeworth Industries," a mechanical voice intoned.

"Miss Beverly Harris," Felicia said as calmly as she could.

"One moment please," the female voice replied, as if she had repeated that same phrase dozens of times a day for several years.

Felicia waited. She crooked her chin over the phone and nestled it snugly between her shoulder and cheek to free both hands so she could pick at the cuticle of her fingernail.

When she heard a click, her hand flew back to the phone, and she sat at attention in her chair.

"Beverly Harris," a woman's voice identified herself. The tone was professional but warm.

"T-this is Felicia Farr," Felicia began. Why hadn't she rehearsed what she would say? Impulsively, she had dialed the number without giving any thought to the conversation. "Uh, I teach at San Pedro High School. My principal, Mr. Humbolt, said you called about a summer job."

"A job?" Miss Harris asked.

"Yes, for an interpreter. Someone who speaks Castilian Spanish," Felicia added.

"Oh, yes. 'Miss Farr' did you say your name was?" Immediately the dawn of recognition warmed the secretary's voice to a friendly, conversational tone. "Yes, I did call. Would you be able to come to the office? I'd like you to fill out an application, and Mr. Bonner wants to interview you."

"Certainly," Felicia agreed, trying to sound interested but not overly eager. "When would you like me to come?"

"How about this afternoon? Say, three o'clock?"

"Fine. I'll be there."

"Good. See you then."

Felicia found it impossible to down any lunch. She sat in her compact kitchen, watching the clock on the wall smirk at her as it slowed its hands down to a turtle's pace.

"You just wait," she threatened the timepiece. "Next time you need to be oiled, don't come crying to me to take you to the repair shop!"

To pass the time, she hunted through her closet for just the right outfit. She rejected several dresses she had bought especially for the classroom. They didn't look professional enough for the business world, she decided. Finally, she settled on a pale cream-colored suit with a light blue blouse. With her hair knotted into a chignon on the back of her head and a subtle covering of makeup coupled with a touch of mascara, she would look businesslike, reasonably attractive but not glamorous.

At precisely three o'clock, Felicia entered the door pointed out to her by the receptionist. The nameplate on the desk read BEVERLY HARRIS. Behind the neat desk sat a well-dressed woman of about forty. Her dark brown hair was showing a few strands of gray. Tiny lines around her large brown eyes were signposts that her youth lay behind her.

"Miss Farr, I'm so glad you could come." Miss Harris smiled warmly. "Won't you sit down?"

"Thank you," Felicia said, returning the smile. She smoothed her suit and took one of the straight-backed chairs across the desk from Beverly Harris. She was immediately impressed by the plush interior of the office, with its thick carpet, expensive-looking oil paintings on the wall, and several exotic plants placed strategically for a tropical effect.

"We feel very fortunate to have found someone so well qualified for this position," Miss Harris began. "We're opening up a new territory for heavy farm equipment in Spain. Most of our salesmen can speak Spanish to some degree, but since they've picked it up either here from the Hispanics or from travels to

Mexico, they speak some version of Mexican Spanish. Our first contacts with our prospective buyers in Spain are critical, and exacting details of the agreement must be worked out. So, naturally, we must have someone who speaks Castilian Spanish as an interpreter."

"Well, I can certainly do that," Felicia said with no hint of immodesty. "I grew up in Spain."

"Fine," Miss Harris exclaimed. "If you'll fill out this application form, Mr. Bonner, our personnel director, would like to talk with you for a few moments. Actually, it's just a formality. I'm really the one who makes the final decision." The older woman's confidential wink told Felicia she had the job if she wanted it.

Felicia took the paper Miss Harris handed her and rummaged in her purse for a pen. Why hadn't she cleaned the blasted thing out? she wondered. There were tissues, notes about possible jobs, clippings from the newspaper, and paper clips all tangled in a jumbled mess. What an idiot she would be if she were turned down for this job because Miss Harris thought she was too sloppy.

"Here," Miss Harris interrupted Felicia's search.

"Thank you," Felicia said gratefully, taking the pen that was offered.

When she had filled out the short form and handed it back to Miss Harris, Felicia looked at the woman expectantly.

"Is there anything you'd like to know about the job before you see Mr. Bonner?" Miss Harris asked, leaning back in her swivel chair and smiling at Felicia.

"Well, yes. The salary, for one. And how long the job lasts. When I'd be expected to go to Spain, and for how long. . . ." Felicia paused.

"Of course," Miss Harris said sympathetically. She quoted Felicia a salary figure that left the younger woman with a lump in her throat. It was twice what she would draw from her teaching salary for the summer.

41

"The job is a temporary one, just for the rest of the summer. However, if all goes well, it might turn into a permanent position, assuming you'd be willing to give up your teaching career, of course. You'll need to be ready to leave for Spain in two weeks. I can't guarantee just how long you'll be there. You see, Lakeworth Industries is part of a large conglomerate, and once you're in Spain, there may be other branches of the business that will require your services before your return. Of course, all your expenses will be paid, so there's no need for you to rush back . . . unless there's a young man, of course." Miss Harris shot Felicia a knowing glance that said the older woman was well experienced in affairs of the heart.

"No," Felicia said evasively. "I don't have any need to rush back. I can be yours for the summer."

"Fine." Miss Harris smiled broadly. "I'm sure Mr. Bonner will find your credentials quite satisfactory." With that, the woman rose and strode crisply to a side door, where she disappeared.

As Miss Harris had predicted, the interview with Mr. Bonner was a mere formality. Less than thirty minutes later, Felicia was on the highway headed back home, and she was an official employee of Lakeworth Industries.

Felicia lost no time in calling Dr. Ambrewster to tell him the good news. When she sent her first check back home, the doctor could transfer her mother to the appropriate type of facility she needed. Felicia would worry about how to pay for her mother's continuing care later if this job didn't turn out to be permanent. If it did, she could knock off teaching for a year or two to earn the extra money, and once her mother was able to function on her own, she could always go back to teaching. What was important was that for the first time since her return from Spain, Felicia now had distinct possibilities of helping her mother so that Francine might grow well enough to see her.

Felicia spent the next few days preparing for her trip. She had a number of dresses that needed mending, and she realized that some of her outfits were woefully tired from their years of service. She had bought hardly any new dresses when she came back to the States because she lived on a strict budget. But with the prospects of a handsome salary for her summer's work, she decided she had to fill out her wardrobe with a few more-up-to-date clothes so that she would fit the image of Lakeworth Industries. While an interpreter didn't have to look like a fashion plate, she would need to dress in well-designed fashions. So, she swallowed her conscience and treated herself to three new dresses that made her choke when she paid for them.

Next, she decided she should drop Don a note at college and tell him of her plans. She mailed the letter Friday morning, so she was surprised when a knock at her door Friday evening announced Don himself.

"Hi." She smiled. "You couldn't have gotten my letter already."

"Letter?" Don asked, leaning against the doorframe and grinning widely. He reached out and pulled Felicia close to him. His blue eyes were crinkling at the corners. His mouth found hers, and he gave her a warm, gentle kiss.

Felicia's heart pounded. But it wasn't a reaction to Don's kiss. It was due to a memory that stirred in her mind of the kiss of another man—a dark, haunting man who had come into her life uninvited and who had stolen a kiss from her in the parking lot at Carlsbad Caverns. Felicia's cheeks warmed with shame that her thoughts should turn to Roderick Bearstern at a time like this.

"Yes," Felicia said, gently pulling back from Don

43

and leading him into her apartment. He sat beside her on the couch. She looked at him for a long moment. His sandy-colored hair and blue eyes, combined with that boyish look, gave him a clean-cut, appealing quality that Felicia wished desperately she could respond to in the same way she had responded to a man she hated. It didn't make any sense for her pulse to pound and her knees to turn to jelly over someone who represented so much of her hated past. How much more sensible it would be to moon over Don, who was a likable fellow and who was interested in her for herself, not for how much money she could earn for him.

"I found that summer job I've been looking for," she revealed.

"Great!" Don exclaimed. "We'll have to go out and celebrate."

"Well, there won't be much time for that," Felicia said. "I have a lot of packing to do, and . . ."

"Packing?" Don said, a frown gnarling his forehead.

"Yes. You see, I got a job as an interpreter for this company, and I have to go to Spain."

Don looked dismayed. "Spain? For how long?"

"I don't know exactly. I guess it could be the rest of the summer. It was kind of indefinite. But the pay is very good, and you know how desperately I need the money for my mother's treatment. I just couldn't say no, Don."

"Yeah, I guess not," Don conceded slowly. He rubbed his chin with his hand. "You will be able to come home with me for a visit before you leave, won't you?" Don asked. "My parents want to meet you, and I made plans for next weekend."

Felicia's blue eyes avoided Don's face and found a spot in the carpet on which to focus. "I'm sorry, Don. But I have to leave Thursday. I'd love to meet your parents, you know I would. If they're half as nice as you are, I'll be crazy about them. But this job means so much to me, Don. It's not for me; it's for my mother." She threw Don a pleading look that begged him to understand.

"That's what makes it so hard," Don said, a note of resignation in his voice. "How can I insist you forget about this job when the money is intended for such a worthy purpose?"

"I knew you'd understand," Felicia said gratefully. At that moment, a great outpouring of affection for Don filled her heart. Then she turned serious. "It's so important to me, Don, to get my mother well enough so that she'll agree to see me. Do you have any idea how much I would love to invite someone 'home' and mean to my mother's house? It's something you take for granted. But getting to know my mother is something I have to work for. I have so many conflicts and emotional problems over my relationship with her. Until I get this situation taken care of, I'm really not emotionally free for any other . . . involvements."

While Felicia didn't want to be so presumptuous as to verbalize her true thoughts, she knew Don was getting serious about her and that their relationship could eventually blossom into an engagement. However, they were at that stage of courting when both parties understood that they were on the verge of getting serious, though neither had yet said it aloud.

"Felicia, from what you've told me, this situation with your mother could be a very long term affair," Don said, turning her face so that she had to look him in the eyes. "What are you going to do if your mother never gets better? How long is she going to be your top priority?"

"I don't know, Don," Felicia admitted, dropping her gaze. "But she'll never get better without the proper care, and I've got to see that she gets it."

Don took her hands in his and squeezed them gently.

"I'm going to miss you," he said softly. "You'll write, won't you?"

"Of course," she said. "Anyway, you're all tied up with summer school, so you have plenty to keep you out of trouble until I get back." Her eyes twinkled with a touch of humor.

"Yeah," Don said noncommittally.

Felicia tried not to notice the disappointment in Don's tone. While she hated to desert him for the summer, she had to admit that she was looking forward to returning to Spain. She had despised the country when she lived there simply because she felt like an exile. It wasn't until she had returned to the United States that she recognized how much a part of the Spanish life she had become. It was a cultural shock to find herself caught up in the fast-paced American way of doing things. She missed the long, leisurely, late-evening meals she was used to in Spain. The attitude of the people in America was so different. There was a basic sadness and concern for death and dying in Spaniards that was lacking in Americans. Here, people lived their lives as if they thought they would never die. While Americans were friendly, there was a warmth lacking when they engaged in business dealings.

Felicia laughed inwardly. Strange, she thought. She was thinking about Americans as if they were another nationality. She was an American, and the first ten years of her life had given her an American identity that she could never shed. Still, the years spent in Spain had left an indelible mark on her character and personality. And she wanted to return to Spain to recapture some of the old-world flavor that she felt slipping away from her since she had been back in her own country.

The evening with Don was pleasant, if a bit strained. While he had popped in unannounced, it was understood between them that they were not seeing anyone else, even though neither had vocalized the arrangement. In fact, Felicia realized, her entire relationship with Don was based on unspoken assumptions. Neither had made any type of verbal commitment to anything.

To smooth things over, the next day Felicia wrote Don's parents a note expressing regret about the lost weekend but assuring them she'd take a rain check until she returned from Spain.

The next thing she knew, Felicia was on a plane jetting to Europe and an encounter with a fate she never dreamed awaited her.

When her plane reached the outer fringes of Madrid, Felicia began to fidget in her seat. She was eager to see the city of over three million people where she had spent the greater part of her life. As soon as she stepped off the plane, she felt a lump knot tightly in her throat. There was something about the dry air here in the central part of the country that gave Felicia a sensation of strength. Parts of Spain were so rugged and arid that only the hardiest survived, and a certain sense of power came from knowing she had prospered in a country so different from the one where she had been born.

A uniformed man met her at the gate and helped her through customs. Then he led her to a long black limousine and drove expertly through the heavy traffic along Avenida America. On a side street at 122 Calle Serrano stood the Museo de Lazaro Galdiano, with its thirty rooms of paintings, pottery, jewels and other works of art. Felicia had visited the museum several times, and she longed to stop and see it again, but the chauffeur drove determinedly on. So she sighed, sat back and contented herself with a quick look at her former home city from the back window of the fast-moving automobile.

Felicia smiled fondly, nostalgia bringing a gleam to her blue eyes as she sped past the Biblioteca Nacional, the National Library. Here, she had spent many hours reading Spanish classics to divert her thoughts from her emotional torment: *El Cid, La Celestina, El Lazarillo de Tormes,* Galdos' *Doña Perfecta* and, of course, Cervantes' *Don Quixote.* In each work, she had identified with the downtrodden, the misunderstood and the displaced. Perhaps it had been because of her interest in literature that she had become a schoolteacher. The last big landmark she passed before stopping in front of her hotel was the Parque del Retiro, a 353-acre park where she had ambled along the shady paths and sat thinking at the foot of beautiful fountains and imposing statues of Spanish monarchs.

She had been right to accept this job, she realized. She knew she would never live in Spain again. America was her real home now. But she needed this trip back to the country where she had spent so much of her life in order to remind her how desperately she had longed to get to know her mother. She had felt guilty leaving Don the way she had. But it was the right thing to do, she realized now, and being back in Spain erased all the guilt feelings she had been harboring the last several days.

Felicia was soon settled in her comfortable hotel room, with its cool tile floors and its large, cozy bed. Jet lag reared its weary head, and Felicia stretched out on the green velvet bedspread and dozed off to sleep.

Late that afternoon Felicia received a phone call from Tom Undermeyer, the sales representative from Lakeworth Industries who was assigned the Spanish territory. He asked her to arrive at his office the next morning by ten o'clock. That evening she phoned a few friends she knew would want to hear from her and ate supper with her best friend from college.

Felicia spent a week helping Tom Undermeyer iron out the fine points of a complex contract he was working out between Lakeworth Industries and a Spanish company eager to import the latest in heavy farm

machinery. She proved invaluable both as an interpreter and as a mediator, and Tom said he was recom-
mending her for a bonus.

The next part of her assignment took her to Barcelona, the country's greatest industrial center. Situated
on the Mediterranean, Barcelona had a character all its
own. In the heart of the historical Catalonia region, this
part of Spain boasted an ethnic populace with a fierce
pride in its distinctive heritage. A strong rivalry between Madrid and Barcelona had existed for genera-
tions.

Felicia disembarked the plane into a more humid,
gentler climate. A soft breeze fanned her hair. As she
rode a taxi to her hotel, she saw the familiar sights of
street urchins playing on the sidewalks and women
dressed in the black garb of mourning. The driver
turned onto Las Ramblas, a spacious boulevard with
two streets forming a ribbon on each side of a wide
central mall for pedestrians. On each edge of the mall,
open-air booths were manned by vendors offering a
variety of items from newspapers and magazines to
flowers and even live birds. Felicia saw the familiar
rejas, the black iron grillwork that covered many of the
first-floor windows of apartments and shops. A warm,
comfortable feeling stole over her. When she stepped
from the cab, a street vendor offered her a cluster of
fresh grapes, which she bought with *pesetas* recently
converted from her American dollars.

Warm, pungent aromas of old-world foods, the
coastal air and the scent of Spanish flowers mingled into
a fragrance that Felicia recognized as typical of nowhere else in the world except Barcelona. She had
spent many summers in this coastal city. Next to
Madrid, she loved it more than any other city in Spain.

The summer sun shone brightly, warming her skin as
she left the taxi and entered the shady interior of the
hotel. There was a message waiting for her at the front

desk with an address where she was to report the next morning for her subsequent translating assignment.

With the evening free, Felicia decided to amble down Las Ramblas. While not as elaborate as a modern American shopping mall, it had a character that was lacking in the steel and concrete shopping centers found in the New World. The open air, where birds flew overhead and cars sped by, afforded one a fantastic view of every type of architecture available. From tall, majestic skyscrapers of glass and steel to Moorish- and Greek-style structures with an old-world flavor, the buildings along the promenade area spoke of the history of Barcelona, both the old and the new. And the one sight that Felicia loved most of all and had missed most ardently in the United States was the fantasia of flowers that lined both sides of Las Ramblas, turning it into a veritable garden. Dark-eyed women sat beside vases of long-stemmed buds and carefully wrapped a thin wire around clusters of stems to form artistically crafted bouquets. Unable to resist the impulse, Felicia stopped at a flower stand and pointed to a modest floral arrangement, which she held to her nostrils and sniffed dreamily. Ah, Barcelona, she thought. Spain. Would that I could take parts of you with me back to the States.

The sweet fragrance of the blooms brought a smile to Felicia's full lips. She dropped the required *pesetas* into the girl's hand, thanked her and drifted off, her eyes ranging over the Spanish-language magazines, the photo booths, the jewelry and other assorted wares displayed for resident and tourist alike.

She wandered around for quite some time before she realized that the sky was growing dark, and the pink glow of the setting sun lent a special transparent quality to the vendors shutting up their stands for the night and disappearing into the darkness.

Realizing how hungry she was, Felicia located a small, out-of-the-way restaurant, where she found to her delight the menu featured gazpacho, a cold soup of chopped tomato, green pepper and cucumber topped with bread crumbs and seasoned with garlic. While she downed the succulent liquid mixture, the waiter brought to her table a tortilla Española, an omelet she favored above any other kind she had ever eaten. Combined with the customary eggs were bits of sausage, potatoes and onions. She turned down a choice of a sweet Spanish pastry for dessert in favor of locally grown peaches, which made her mouth water from their sweet juice as she bit into the soft flesh.

Back at her hotel, Felicia, unsuspecting of the fate that awaited her the next day, snuggled down comfortably between the cool sheets of her hotel bed and breathed the fragrant aroma of the flowers she had placed on her pillow. Goose bumps popped out on her skin when she pulled the top sheet over her and felt a cold draught of air slip out from between the layers of fabric surrounding her gowned body. She closed her eyes dreamily, her slender fingers clutching the stems of the flowers, and drifted off to sleep.

The next morning, Felicia dressed in her cream-colored suit with the blue blouse that she had worn on her interview at Lakeworth Industries. She hired a taxi to take her to the address left for her in yesterday's message and exited into the bright, warm sun at the foot of a towering glass building in the heart of the central business district. The glare from the building's shiny exterior caused her to squint. What a contrast with the Spanish architecture of the centuries-old structures in some parts of Barcelona, Felicia thought. Ornate archways, splendid statues and masterpieces of artistic work distinguished the classic Spanish buildings from the modern high-rise towers with their impersonal exteriors devoid of everything except row upon row of cold glass windows.

Felicia entered the cool interior of the building and noticed the contrast with people on the street. Outside was a potpourri of old men in straw hats, dowdy women in formless dresses contrasting with men in conservative business suits and small children chattering in high-pitched voices. Inside the building, Felicia saw only smartly dressed professional people, some standing in small clusters in the foyer, speaking in restrained, crisp tones. There was an aura of impersonal importance about these people. Gone were the street smells of crisp, fried fruit in puffy pastry coverings, baskets of blooming flowers, and the dank, lingering aroma of sea air blown in from the harbor. The air inside was sterile, clean and without body. It hung limply in the space between ceiling and floor, neither calling attention to itself nor intruding into the important business transactions being carried on within the walls of this skyscraper.

Felicia took the elevator to the appropriate floor, got off and walked down the carpeted hallway to office number 709. Her shoulder purse swung lazily from side to side as she strode over to the desk and told the receptionist that she was reporting for duty. She waited only five minutes before being shown into an inner office, which turned out to be a photographer's studio.

Felicia took an overstuffed chair next to an enormous desk flanked by several rows of large file cabinets. To her left there was a divider wall, which only partly concealed a large camera on a tripod and a backdrop of soft pink.

Felicia shifted nervously in her chair and began to pick the cuticles of her nails. Anything resembling professional photography unnerved her. It was this kind of setup that had robbed her of her rightful access to her mother, and she didn't like the thought of serving as an interpreter under such circumstances. Maybe the assignment would be a short one, she reassured herself. She would fulfill her duties and move on quickly to something else for the company. She didn't quite see the connection between heavy farm machinery and photography, but maybe this studio was used to photograph brochures of some of the smaller machinery.

Felicia heard a click and looked up to see the door of the office opening. Her eyes were not prepared for the message they carried to her brain. No, she screamed silently. It can't be!

"Well, I see you're on time," he said casually, as if she had expected to see Roderick Bearstern stride through the office door.

Felicia sat stunned. Vaguely, she heard a thud. She realized dimly that she had dropped her purse on the floor. Her hand had become so limp that it could no longer support the weight dangling from her palm by the strap.

"Y-you!" she choked.

"In the flesh," he said crisply. His brown eyes danced mirthfully. A glitter of amusement flashed from the green flecks sprinkled in the brown irises as Roderick Bearstern's strong jaw muscles relaxed and a grin spread across his face. He walked casually to the dark desk and sat on its corner, towering over Felicia. He rested his palms on his legs and bent down slightly. She recoiled from the scent of his musky after shave lotion and the warmth of his body as the space between them collapsed.

A rushing sound in her ears told her that her pulse was racing. She gripped the arms of the chair to steady the trembling of her hands. Her mouth went dry and cottony.

"I told you you'd be mine, Felicia Farr," Roderick

reminded her, a wicked glimmer flashing from his dark eyes. "And sooner than you thought."

"What kind of an underhanded trick is this, anyway?" Felicia demanded through taut lips. Her body was rigid with anger. "How did you bribe Lakeworth Industries to send me here? And what are you doing in Spain?"

"I didn't bribe anybody," Roderick chuckled. "Except maybe you. I own Lakeworth Industries."

"W-what?" Felicia gasped. She slumped back in the chair, her shattered thoughts scattered into thousands of fragments that she couldn't piece back together. None of this made any sense.

Roderick straightened up, his broad shoulders blocking out the ceiling light behind him. Felicia hadn't realized at their first meeting how truly strong and imposing a man he was. And neither had she given him enough credit for determination. She hàd grossly underestimated just how much he really wanted her and the lengths he was willing to go to in order to satisfy his desire for her.

"Yes," he continued, "as I told you, I am the president and chairman of the board of a large holding company that has several businesses. It's a conglomerate. It includes both the farm machinery company and Magic Glo Cosmetics, among many others."

"But," she protested, still not wanting to believe that she was actually an employee of this man, "it's just too much of a coincidence that I would have landed a job with a company you own."

"Hardly a coincidence," he said casually, as if he were used to arranging secret networks of underhanded operations every day. "You forget that my company contacted you, indirectly."

"That's right," Felicia conceded.

"I knew you needed money, so it was a simple matter to have Lakeworth Industries call your principal and tell them they were looking for a translator of Castilian Spanish.

"It all looked so innocent," Felicia muttered.

"Precisely," Roderick agreed. "You hadn't the slightest suspicion that your assignment, back to the country where you grew up, would send you right into my arms, did you?"

Felicia stiffened at his words. She bit her tongue in anger at herself for allowing a mental picture to flash by—a mental picture of her in Roderick Bearstern's arms.

Felicia quickly diverted the conversation away from talk about physical contact with Roderick Bearstern, even symbolically.

"I was told my job would be serving as translator for a transaction involving heavy farm machinery. I did not agree to translate for you," she said coldly.

"True," Roderick drawled slowly, in a tone that said he was baiting her. He paused. "However, I must point out that you were told the job might entail interpreting assignments for other branches of the company."

"Don't try to patronize me," Felicia retorted. "This is a photography studio. It's very clear what you have in mind. You thought you could trick me into posing for you."

"Nothing of the sort," Roderick said in a feigned hurt voice that made Felicia's blood boil. "It so happens that I'm overseeing some advertising photos on location here in Spain for a new campaign for Magic Glo. And I need an interpreter."

"If you went to the trouble of tracking me down and offering me this job through my school back home, you obviously had in mind more than just interpreting duties," Felicia said tartly. "Just how did you find me in the first place?" she demanded.

Roderick shrugged at her accusation. Then he explained. "Your mother was a very special woman,

Felicia," Roderick said huskily. "She had an aura about her that captured the imagination of the public as no other woman has in years."

"Yeah, I know," Felicia said impatiently. "You told me all that already."

"About a year ago, I was looking through some old magazines, and I came across some photographs of your mother advertising Magic Glo cosmetics. While the makeup and hairstyle were a little dated, your mother's charm and appeal were as vibrant as ever. I realized that since your mother left the business, there have been many models who have flashed on the scene briefly, but there's been nobody who had the staying power of your mother. Year after year she adorned billboards, magazine covers—"

"Yeah, I know," Felicia said bitterly, remembering the years in Spain that that popularity had imposed on her. "She was everybody's favorite sweetheart for almost as long as I can remember."

"Well," Roderick continued, "I talked to my father about trying to find another model with the unique qualities of your mother. He said that it was too bad Francine Farr's daughter had been shipped away to Spain. We had a successor to the throne, but no one knew where you were."

"Why didn't you just ask my mother?" Felicia queried.

"Because she won't see me—or anybody for that matter. So I hired a private detective to track you down. It took awhile, and by the time we located you, you were teaching in New Mexico. I came into the classroom that night to see whether you had inherited any of your mother's special qualities, whether you had that same magic spark that made your mother America's top model for Magic Glo Cosmetics for so many years."

Felicia hated to admit it to herself, but curiosity as to Roderick Bearstern's assessment of her burned in her.

"And?" she said haughtily, as if the answer would surely bore her.

"I followed you to Carlsbad, didn't I?" he said. "I asked you to pose for me, didn't I?"

Crimson circles appeared on Felicia's cheeks as she realized her obvious female vanity. While she had never tried to maximize her appeal, she did like to think of herself as desirable, as any normal woman would. Embarrassment sealed her lips, and the air hung silent as Roderick sauntered to the file cabinet, opened it deftly and extracted a folder.

"Here," he said, tossing the folder on the desk.

The smack of the paper on wood caused Felicia's eyes to instinctively dart in the direction of the sound.

"Look at these," he ordered.

Curiosity, coupled with suspicion, chiseled shallow furrows in Felicia's brow. Gingerly, she picked up the folder. Then she put it back down on the desk—unopened.

"I've seen these," she said flatly.

"No you haven't," Roderick corrected her. "They are not the same pictures I showed you before. Look at them!"

Her fingers responded to his commanding tone. She opened the folder, and for the second time that morning she gasped.

"Why, they're photographs of me," she declared, as she flipped through the pictures showing her leaving her apartment, walking to school, coming out of the grocery store. "You had no right!" she exploded, tossing the pictures on the desk and jumping to her feet.

"Relax," he said soothingly. "There's nothing illegal about what I did. I simply took a few photographs of a prospective model without her knowledge. These are not for sale and will never be published."

"But it's an invasion of my privacy!" she snapped.

"No, it's not," Roderick countered. He walked over, put his hands on her shoulders and pressured her back into her chair. A bolt of electricity shot through her at his touch and the nearness of his body to hers. She told herself her reaction was due entirely to anger, but a strange little voice whispered something in her ear that she couldn't quite make out, and she sat down feeling puzzled and confused.

"If I had offered you the chance to revive the image of Francine Farr, and your photographs hadn't turned out promising, think how disappointed you would have been. I assumed you would jump at the chance to make top dollar and become a model. So, I took a few preliminary shots of you to see how photogenic you are before I approached you."

"And if I had failed your little screen test?" Felicia asked sharply.

"Then you would never have been the wiser," he said.

"Thanks for the consideration," she said testily. "It warms my heart that you were so concerned about not disappointing me."

Roderick merely laughed at the venom in her words, and that just made her angrier.

"The photos were pretty good," Roderick went on. "But I didn't take them myself. I hired a photographer. So, I decided the only sure way to find out what kind of charm you exude was to see you in person and find out for myself."

"And that's why you invaded my classroom," she said.

"I would hardly call it an invasion." He laughed in the superior manner of his that infuriated Felicia.

"It was an uncalled-for intrusion," Felicia pointed

out. "That was a PTA meeting for parents of students in that school. You were an outsider. You had no business there."

"I didn't bother anybody," Roderick defended himself.

"You bothered *me!*" she said frostily.

"Oh?" Roderick grinned broadly. "Did I now?"

"Not like that!" she said hotly, and the little voice whispered in her ear again, confusing her a second time. Stop that! she muttered to the invisible body the voice occupied.

Felicia immediately changed the subject. "If you were satisfied with the way I looked, why did you bother to follow me to Carlsbad?"

"I decided I needed another look," Roderick said. "After all, you were in that drab school setting, wearing that unflattering hairstyle, those schoolteacher clothes and amateurish makeup."

"I was dressed quite appropriately for the occasion," Felicia defended herself, tears stinging her eyes.

"I wanted to see you away from the school setting," Rod went on, ignoring her comment. "I had my detective check up on you, and I found you were helping sponsor a trip to Carlsbad, so I followed you to get a closer look at you in different surroundings. I again liked what I saw, so I decided to approach you about a modeling job."

Felicia scrupulously avoided mention of the kiss Roderick Bearstern had stolen from her, but her heart leaped in her chest at the memory of his hands on her skin, his mouth crushing down on hers.

"You know my feelings about that," she said sharply.

Slowly, Roderick approached her, his brown eyes burning into her blue ones. She averted her gaze. As her eyes trailed down toward the floor, they passed over his broad shoulders, down the expensive tie covering the front of his Italian shirt, and took in the drape of his trouser legs around his muscular thighs. She shivered at her own response, for no matter how much she hated Roderick Bearstern, the sight of him made her nerves tingle and her blood race.

"I know what you told me," Roderick said knowingly, implying there was more to her refusal than she had admitted.

She dared to look him in the face once again, and her breath caught in her throat. "I told you the truth!" she retorted.

"You told me what you want to believe is the truth," Roderick corrected her. "But there's more to your refusal than your being worried that you might be exploited as a model. After all, your mother could have refused unreasonable work assignments. She could have insisted on keeping you with her. But she was not strong willed enough to stand up to your stepfather. No matter what profession she had been in, he would have used and abused her. It's not modeling that ruined your life, Felicia, and you know it."

"That's not true!" Felicia erupted.

"Then prove me wrong," Roderick challenged arrogantly.

"No," Felicia whispered from a hollow place in her chest.

"Then you're no stronger than your mother," Roderick said in a condemning tone. "You're afraid that if you find out the truth about modeling, you'll want to model after all. Then you won't be able to harbor the same bitterness toward your mother. It will force you to quit feeling sorry for yourself, something you don't want to do because you enjoy making yourself miserable."

"No!" Felicia fumed. "That's not true. You don't know what you're talking about. You're trying to trick me."

"Search your feelings," Roderick instructed her authoritatively. "You'll find I'm right."

The tone of Roderick's command captured Felicia's attention, and her eyes met his across a blistering expanse of arid space. There was a mastery in his gaze that unnerved her and made her want to avert her eyes. But she couldn't. His brown eyes, piercing through her wavering blue gaze, seemed to reach into her very being, to the depths of her shrinking soul, and forcefully draw out from her a part of herself that she had refused to believe existed. It was a battle for her to retain possession of her senses. So strong was his magnetic strength that she felt surely she would lose complete control of her inner self to this man. It was as if his probing were revealing every hidden corner of her secret life, the private thoughts that everyone has that belong to the thinker and to her alone.

A scarlet haze passed over Felicia's cheeks as she realized how cleverly Roderick Bearstern had penetrated into her mental lair.

"You don't know what you're talking about!" Felicia choked.

"Then why are you so afraid to give it a try?" Roderick demanded. "It wouldn't take long to find out if I've read you right. After I located you in that bland teaching job, I had my company conduct a market survey. The name Francine Farr is almost as well known today as it was during her heyday." Roderick's eyes began to glow, the green flecks casting glimmers that Felicia recognized. She had seen that same expression on men's faces before when they had talked of her mother.

"Hers is one of those legendary names people still talk about in hushed whispers. A Francine Farr revival, via the daughter, Felicia Farr, would be a sure winner," Roderick said enthusiastically. Now he was talking to a phantom in the air, as if he and his memories were alone in the room. Then he turned his attention to Felicia again. "It wouldn't take you long to find out what modeling is really like," he said in a more down-to-earth tone of voice. "You've got your mother's reputation to build on. If you've got what it takes, your career will shoot off like a skyrocket. I'd handle you personally. Of all the companies in my holdings, my favorites are the cosmetic lines. That's where the big money is. Besides, I like personally supervising the selection and promotion of my top models." Roderick's eyes skimmed over Felicia's frame and brought an angry blush to her cheeks.

"Can't you take no for an answer?" Felicia retorted. "I'm not about to trade in on my mother's name!"

"So that's it!" Roderick said brightly. A smirk crossed his lips. "You're afraid of the competition. It's not really that you fear and hate the kind of person modeling might turn you into. You're refusing because you think you can't possibly live up to your mother's glamorous image. You're afraid you'll be compared to your mother and will come up wanting!"

"No! No! No!" Felicia protested, her vision blurred by a fresh surge of tears. She rose to her feet, grabbed her purse and shot Roderick a murderous glance. "Just who do you think you are, with your armchair psychology, anyway?" she demanded. "You don't know me. You have no idea how I feel, unless you've had your spies somehow picking my brains with some sort of super-snooping mind readers. Considering all the sneaky tactics you've used so far, I wouldn't put anything past you!" she snapped. She turned on her heel and marched toward the door.

"Just a minute, Felicia," Roderick said smoothly, in a tone that said he still had the upper hand. "Remember, you're still working for me."

"No I'm not!" she said triumphantly. "I quit!"

"And how do you propose to get home?" Roderick asked blandly.

A frown crossed Felicia's brow. "What do you mean?" She stopped and turned toward him, a suspicious look on her face.

"I paid your expenses from the States," he pointed out, "and I'll pay your fare home. But only after you've completed the work I brought you here to do. I hired you as an interpreter, and I insist you complete your obligation to me."

"But you tricked me!" she complained bitterly.

"Call it what you will, you agreed to work for the entire summer, if necessary, as an interpreter, and I am holding you to that agreement."

A black anger smothered Felicia's protests. She was stuck and she knew it. Until she drew at least her first month's salary, she didn't have a penny of her own money. She had arranged for her summer teaching salary to be mailed directly to her bank account, so there was no way she could get her hands on any money fast. She was living in Spain on the expense account of Lakeworth Industries, and Roderick could cancel that in five seconds.

"I'll see you in the morning," Roderick said coolly, gloating over her defeat.

Wordlessly, Felicia turned toward the door. She threw her purse strap over her shoulder, flung open the door and marched out.

"Roderick Bearstern, you'll pay for this!" she growled through clenched teeth.

Chapter Four

"I can't believe I'm doing this," Felicia grumbled to herself as she stepped off the open-air tram at the north side of the Plaza de Cataluña, Barcelona's largest square. She walked past the large, imposing bank just across the street from the plaza and stood under one of the tall trees, where a soft breeze teased the few strands of hair dangling loosely around her face. The rest of her blond locks were caught up in the chignon on the back of her head. She wore a cool summer dress of light green cotton and polyester, and white sandals, the straps of which lashed around her trim ankles like a slave bracelet. It was an appropriate designation, for at this point Felicia felt herself a slave.

"Imagine my working for Roderick Bearstern and interpreting for some model that he's exploiting the way his father did my mother," Felicia said aloud in bewilderment. A passing Spaniard shot Felicia a strange glance as she walked across the street muttering to herself. She was so upset that she failed to enjoy her renewed acquaintance with the beautiful park. This area gave the people of Barcelona a refreshing break from the forest of tall buildings that dominated this part of the city near the port.

Roderick had called her yesterday after she had reached her hotel and had told her where to meet him for this morning's shooting assignment. He was going to break in a new model, Cheryl Singer, who was posing for a series of ads and commercials for a new perfume with a Spanish name and image. The first still shots were to be made against the park background, showing some of the many statues, the archways, and the twin fountains that bubbled gaily in the center of a lawn bordered by a narrow sidewalk.

"Don't count on my being there!" Felicia had said hotly.

"You'll be there," Roderick had laughed in that confident, infuriating manner that made her vow she would starve before she'd work another minute for that man.

But this morning she had awakened in a different frame of mind. If she didn't complete her assignment, Roderick could refuse to pay her, and he certainly wouldn't let her work in any other branch of the company to finish out the summer. If she didn't show up for work, she jeopardized her mother's chance to receive the kind of medical care she needed. So, reluctantly, Felicia had retrieved the address from the trash can where she had thrown it.

Felicia's high heels clicked across the cement inlaid with tile as she crossed the large multicolored circle in the center of the square. Several elderly people sat dreamily staring out into space as Felicia headed toward a large statue of a man and horse where the film crew was scheduled to meet.

She rounded a cluster of trees and spotted a black camera set up on a tripod. It was aimed in the general direction of the statue. A small, dark man with gleaming black eyes and a little bottlebrush moustache was twisting a silver knob on one side of the camera.

"Felicia," Roderick said when he saw her. "I knew you'd make it." The confident glitter in his brown eyes infuriated her. It wasn't bad enough that she had to work for this man, but she had to put up with his arrogance, too.

"I didn't have anything better to do," she tossed at him.

"I'd like you to meet Juan Carlos," he said, ignoring her remark as if it had meant nothing. He led her to the small man, who stepped from behind the camera and smiled broadly at her.

"Juan Carlos, Felicia Farr," Roderick said.

"Glad to meet you," Felicia said in Spanish.

"The pleasure is all mine," Juan Carlos said in Spanish, bowing from the waist. "And how glad I am that you are here. Señor Bearstern needs your fluent tongue. I speak no English, and he speaks so little Spanish that we end up gesturing to each other in sign language."

"Besides," Felicia guessed, "I imagine he speaks Mexican Spanish, like most Americans."

"I would hardly say he speaks it at all." Juan Carlos chuckled. "So far I have understood almost nothing he has said."

Roderick stood looking at the two of them with an expressionless face. Then his eyes began to sparkle as he gazed over Felicia's shoulder.

"Cheryl," he called, waving his arm over his head. Felicia turned to squint behind her, her hand shading her face from the rays of the morning sun streaming between the tops of the tall buildings across the street.

Walking toward them with an entourage of admirers

and a retinue of makeup artists and fashion specialists came a willowy brunette. Her long curly hair cascaded down her back and played around milk-white shoulders draped gracefully with tiny gold straps that held up a puffy gold dress, which swirled around the woman's tapered calves. Large blue eyes were shaded artfully by a contrasting eye shadow. Her pouty mouth was etched with a shimmering rose lipstick. She was very thin, model slender, and wore her dress like a queen. She had the captivating good looks of a woman who knew what she wanted out of life and was determined to get it—and on her own terms.

Felicia didn't care that she looked absolutely dowdy compared to Cheryl Singer. After all, she wasn't interested in standing before the cameras and selling her soul to America for the price of a mink coat. Regardless of what Roderick Bearstern said, she had very sound reasons for her decision not to follow in her mother's glamorous footsteps.

"Oh, Roderick," Cheryl pouted, "I look just dreadful this morning. Can't we postpone this session until later? I'm positive I saw a red vessel in my eye this morning. I don't want my first pictures to be marred. I never should have let you talk me into staying up so late," she purred naughtily. She walked up to Roderick, ignoring everyone else, and gave him a pitiful look.

"Let me see," Rod said solicitously. He peered into Cheryl's face for a long minute. "Yes, I see what you mean," he agreed in a tone that showed he was patronizing her. Apparently she didn't catch the undercurrent, because she opened her eyes wide and stood looking serious while Roderick finished the examination.

"I'm sure we can touch that up in the darkroom."

"Are you positive?" Cheryl whined.

"Of course," Roderick reassured her. "You'll look

just as lovely as always. You have the potential to be a big model, Cheryl," he told her, glancing at Felicia with a haughty look on his face. "I'll make sure your photos show you off to your best advantage."

"Oh, thank you, Roderick," Cheryl cooed, and Felicia felt herself grow nauseated. Cheryl gave the air a pouty kiss in Roderick's direction and sighed. "Then I guess I'm ready," she said, puffing her hair out over her shoulders.

The retinue of people took up posts to form a crescent behind Juan Carlos, and Roderick began issuing orders. Two people were assigned to hold off gawkers. The makeup mistress hovered just outside the camera's range to touch up any shiny spots that might break through Cheryl's makeup. And two assistants positioned electronic flashes to wash away any shadows that might distort Cheryl's features.

"Oh, Roderick, it's so hot," Cheryl complained as he led her to a spot just to the left of the statue.

"We won't be here long," he reassured her. "We'll do some of the shots in the studio and superimpose your image over the background. We've got to find the best combination of light and scenery to sell the perfume," he reminded her. "And right now, we don't know just what that is. We won't know it until we see it, so I'm going to have Juan Carlos take plenty of shots of you. You just listen to me and do what I tell you. Okay?"

Cheryl gave a little sullen pout before nodding.

"Felicia," Roderick said, adopting a very business-like tone. "Tell Juan Carlos that we want shots of Cheryl when she's looking sultry. Her best expression is when her chin is titled down just slightly and she's looking up at the camera."

Felicia translated, and Juan Carlos nodded and smiled.

"Isn't it awfully hard giving instructions through a

translator?" Felicia asked. "Wouldn't it be easier to take the photos yourself?"

"If I had to deal with an ordinary photographer, it would be," Roderick said. "But Juan Carlos has a reputation for being the best in Spain . . . maybe the world. I've seen his work many times. There's no substitute for an artistic man behind the camera. Give him a model like your mother, and they can set the modeling world on its ear."

"Okay, Cheryl," Roderick instructed, "let me see that look of desire on your face. Tell me with your eyes that you want me."

Cheryl tossed back her head and then titled it forward, her long black hair tumbling over her milky shoulders. She pouted, twisted, turned and emoted silently while Roderick called out phrases to conjure up in her the sensual feeling he hoped she could translate into a look that would sell the latest line of perfume in the Magic Glo line.

The camera clicked repeatedly, and Cheryl began playing up to it more and more.

Roderick became absorbed in the scene, as if he had a passion for this kind of work. His voice grew husky and thick as he lured from Cheryl the best she had to give.

He told Felicia he wanted to capture on film the innocent, naive quality in Cheryl, and Felicia translated to Juan Carlos what expression to look for while Roderick made verbal love to Cheryl.

Felicia had to turn away. It was obscene the way Cheryl looked at Roderick and tried to seduce him and the millions of people that would see her photographs if she became a top model. It was a different aura from the one her mother had projected. While Cheryl worked at being blatantly sexy, Felicia's mother had possessed a rare combination of class, charm and sensuality, coupled with an innocent expression that gave her a wholesome sex appeal, which held a magic allure for both men and women. It was this spark that set her mother miles ahead of the closest contender in the modeling world.

Cheryl Singer was undoubtedly pretty, but she obviously traded on her looks, and that impression would come across in the photographs. Francine Farr had been beautiful, but it was a beauty that transcended mere sexuality. She had style. But it was a natural, unassuming style that she had had from birth. It had glittered forth from her photographs and had made her unique.

"Please, Roderick," Cheryl pleaded after Juan Carlos had clicked rapidly with his automatic drive attachment to the camera that was capable of snapping several frames per second. "It's getting so hot. Don't you think we've done enough for this morning?" The makeup lady scurried forward and dabbed Cheryl's nose with a large puff.

"Just one more roll," Roderick promised, "and we'll finish the rest in the studio."

Cheryl stuck out her full bottom lip and wrinkled her chin with displeasure, but she stood rooted to the spot.

Roderick walked slowly from side to side, eyeing Cheryl from several angles, his brown eyes narrowing into slits as he scrutinized her.

"Tell Juan Carlos that I want a slightly different angle," Roderick said thoughtfully. He indicated where he wanted the camera placed, and Felicia translated.

Juan Carlos frowned but moved the camera. Then he peered through the viewfinder and began shaking his head. "No," he said solemnly. "This angle makes her features appear hard."

Felicia repeated the observation in English to Roderick, who came around, looked in the camera for himself and concluded that he wanted to try it anyway.

Juan Carlos protested, declaring that he would never

allow such a photograph of his to be used. He argued that he did not want to ruin his reputation. Felicia started to translate, but apparently the tone of his voice made his message quite clear, because Roderick began his counterargument before she had finished.

Felicia was startled by the angry outburst between the two men and once refused to translate a volley of colorful insults. As their voices grew louder and more threatening, she began to shrink back and to speak more softly, her voice catching in her throat.

Just as she was sure they were going to come to blows, the sudden storm died, and Roderick and Juan Carlos began to smile at each other. Felicia stood shaken by the emotional earthquake. Her hands grew damp, and her throat became dry. Her eyes darted from the large, imposing man to the small, artistic one, and she feared the amenitites were the preliminaries for a verbal dual or maybe even a physical one. But when Juan Carlos crouched behind the camera and readied himself for more camera work, Felicia breathed a heavy sigh and realized the temper tantrum was over. And that's all it was, after all.

Men! she thought. If two women had allowed themselves to reach that kind of arm-waving, name-calling state, they surely would have ended up pulling hair, scratching and flailing their arms in wild attempts to land blows to the other's body. But men could race to the precipice of a knock-down, drag-out brawl and suddenly retreat, as if nothing had happened.

Soon the shooting came to an end, and Roderick promised Cheryl lunch at an expensive Spanish restaurant before the afternoon's shooting session.

"Oh, wonderful," Cheryl bubbled. "I'm famished."

"Just watch what you order," Roderick warned. "Mustn't put any fat on that great frame of yours."

A bitter taste gurgled up in Felicia's throat at Roderick's admonition. Nothing had changed since her mother had been a model with Magic Glo Cosmetics. Didn't Cheryl realize how she was being used? The poor girl thought she had Roderick Bearstern dangling from puppet strings on her fingers. But in reality, she was the puppet, and he the puppeteer. She would live her life according to his rules and his time schedule. She would eat what he told her to eat, wear what he picked out and attend parties he thought good for her career. As a matter of fact, if he wanted her to, she would be his mistress. And from all indications, that was just what he wanted.

"Join us for lunch?" Roderick asked Felicia and Juan Carlos.

Cheryl knitted her eyebrows negatively and gave Rod's arm a sudden tug, but he ignored her.

"No," Felicia said caustically, her stomach becoming more queasy by the minute. How could Cheryl prostitute herself like that, Felicia's conscience screamed. It was indecent!

"I'll go," Juan Carlos replied when Felicia translated the offer. "But I have to break down this camera equipment first."

Roderick and Juan Carlos agreed on a time and place to meet, and the couple left.

"It was nice meeting you, Juan Carlos," Felicia replied. "I guess I'll see you this afternoon at the studio."

"Yes, I'll be there," Juan Carlos replied as he twisted a knob that released the camera from its place atop the tripod. "I wouldn't miss this opportunity of working for Señor Bearstern."

"You mean, you like him?" Felicia asked, surprise edging her voice. "After that terrible fight you just had with him?"

"Oh, that was nothing." Juan Carlos smiled, stepping into the shade of a large tree to retrieve a black case. "Just professional pride. I feel very lucky to get this assignment. Not all photographers would agree with me, however."

"What do you mean?" Felicia asked, as Juan Carlos opened the case and began to lovingly place his equipment in it.

"Roderick Bearstern stirs up strong emotions in those who work for him." Juan Carlos chuckled. "Sidney Sveingold, who is one of the best in Europe, would die before he'd work with Roderick. But I say Sidney is a donkey."

Curiosity melted some of Felicia's animosity toward Roderick, and she found herself wanting to know more, in spite of the fact that she had assured herself she didn't care enough about him to bother to question anyone about him. "Why do you say that?" Felicia heard herself asking.

"Because Roderick Bearstern is a genius. Some of my colleagues refuse to work with him because they say Roderick is dictatorial, that he should leave the photography to them, and that he interferes with their work."

"From what I witnessed just a few minutes ago, I should think they are right and that you'd agree with them," Felicia commented.

"That's because you don't understand my philosophy," Juan Carlos said, closing the camera case and standing up to his full height of five-foot-four. "See that building over there?" he said, pointing to an ornate tower peeking through the cluster of more modern structures almost blocking it from view.

"Yes."

"That building could have been planned by one man. If it had, all its designs would have been the product of one mind, of one imagination. We would not have the beautiful, elaborately ornate edifice you now see, because no one man can dream all the intricacies that are stored in the minds of many. But that building delights us today because it is the product of the best minds of its day. The greatest artists shared their best and fought for their own ideas to go into that structure. And we, the beneficiaries of that blending of the best art of a former time, have a rich treasure because one man's ego did not dominate."

"And you feel the same way about your photography?" Felicia concluded.

"Exactly," Juan Carlos agreed. "You see, photographing a beautiful woman, for whatever purpose, is an art. I have my ideas and they are excellent. It is not without modesty that I tell you I am one of the most famous photographers in the world. And my reputation is well deserved. But I am so well recognized because I admit I have limitations, and I am willing to learn from others. No one ever knows all there is to know about an art form, in spite of what Sveingold thinks."

"In other words, you believe in picking other people's brains?" Felicia asked.

"Yes. Why not? Roderick has an indefinable quality about him that brings out the best in his models. He has a flawless eye for picking the right clothes for each woman. He even sets up his top models in a luxurious lifestyle that adds a touch of casual elegance to their demeanor. And all that comes through on film. By myself, I can produce excellent photographs, but with someone like Roderick Bearstern, those same pictures reach heights that can only be described as superb. Well, why shouldn't I work with him? It takes nothing away from me."

"It sounds to me as if you're saying you gain from working with him," Felicia observed.

"I do," Juan Carlos said. "While I may disagree with him sometimes, he generates an excitement that spurs me to greater heights. When I think I have seen all of a model's expressions and have photographed the best she has to offer, Roderick Bearstern can turn her on a little more every time and draw from her more than she herself realizes she has." Juan Carlos' eyes took on an admiring look, as if he were speaking of some supreme guru, and Felicia realized for the first time what high-class company she was keeping.

Whatever his critics or admirers thought of him, Roderick Bearstern obviously was tops in his business. Grudgingly, she had to admit a certain admiration for his ability. But that didn't mean she had to like him. Barracudas were great swimmers, but she wouldn't want to inhabit the same waters with them.

Felicia and Juan Carlos chatted only a few minutes more before they parted company. Felicia found a small sidewalk café, where she enjoyed her solitude while she ate a savory lunch of *paella,* a casserole of rice, saffron, peas and pimiento mixed with chunks of chicken and seafood. It was wonderful to taste the authentic food of Spain again. She had time before the afternoon shooting schedule to browse among the many shops, and she felt a twinge when she saw a bullfight poster prominently displayed in one window. It was the one thing about Spain she did not miss. While aficionados had tried their best to explain to her the beauty and pagentry of the *corrida,* as it was called, she had never been able to divorce herself from feeling sorry for the bull.

As she strolled along in the warm sun, with a light film of perspiration beading on her forehead, Felicia battled thoughts about Roderick Bearstern that fought for recognition in her mind. She had decided long ago that he was ruthless. His Francine Farr revival was so important to him, he didn't give a snap about Felicia's feelings. But she hadn't, until today, realized there was more to him than just a cold, calculating mind. Juan Carlos had opened her eyes to another side of Roderick Bearstern she hadn't known existed. It was hard for Felicia to admit she could feel any admiration for a man like Roderick. But she couldn't lie to herself any longer. In spite of how much she loathed him and all he stood for, she had too much respect for artistry to deny that he did indeed have a touch of genius when it came to his work. It frightened her that there was any aspect of this man's character that appealed to her, for somewhere in the deep recesses of her mind, she realized vaguely she must steel herself against him. Without wanting to focus on the reality of the thought, Felicia understood at some instinctive level that if she allowed her feelings for Roderick Bearstern to soften an inch, for any reason, she was letting herself in for real trouble.

The afternoon shooting session was much like the morning session had been, except this time the photographs were taken indoors. Cheryl pouted and purred her way around Roderick, while Felicia rolled her eyes in disgust. Again, Roderick talked soothingly and seductively to Cheryl, calling out names of endearment, telling her how absolutely splendid she looked and how fantastic she was. Cheryl writhed in delight, her pouty lips curling up sensuously. She threw her shoulders from side to side, twirled and tossed her shining black hair out behind her, looked out from under her mascaraed lids and licked her lips to give them that moist, come-hither sheen. She continually swung her arms and hips in rhythm to Roderick's vocal orchestrations.

Meanwhile, Felicia translated a few terse directions to Juan Carlos, but the two men seemed to have established a working rapport between them that called for little discussion. Juan Carlos worked the camera masterfully.

Felicia recognized that Roderick's behavior was merely part of his job, to draw out the moods and facial expressions and body stances he knew were a part of Cheryl's repertoire. But the tilt of Cheryl's head, the cocky look in her eyes when she deigned to glance at Felicia and the sensual way she moved her body in response to Roderick's commands triggered unwanted images in Felicia's mind that she tried to blot out.

Theirs was more than just a business relationship, Felicia felt sure. After work, when Roderick and Cheryl were alone . . . *No!* her mind fumed. *Don't think about it.*

But why should she care? she wondered miserably. After all, she couldn't stand Roderick Bearstern. The fact that he was arrogant, conceited, opinionated and domineering, not to mention ruthless and sly, should be enough to make any woman steer clear of him. And yet, she couldn't deny the powerful animal magnetism of the man, the charge of electricity she felt in his presence, the trembling in her whole body he set off just by touching her.

So what? she mumbled silently to herself. That really wasn't so unusual. Lots of men had made her feel that way before. She was sure of it. Only, right now she couldn't think of any of their names. Or remember any of their faces. Or recall anything they had done to-gether. But she was sure they had existed . . . somewhere. . . . Was it really only in her imagination?

When the shooting was over, Cheryl made another one of her adroit attempts to seduce Roderick to ignore Felicia.

"We'll shoot again tomorrow here in the studio," Roderick said. Cheryl had wrapped herself around his arm and was trailing her red fingernails along the back of his large hand. Curly black hairs wilted under her touch and snapped back into place after her fingers had passed them by. Felicia felt her heart flutter for some unexplained reason.

"I'm awfully tired," Cheryl pouted. "I need a long, hot bath and then a massage." She shot Felicia a haughty smirk that announced Roderick was her territory. "You do give the best back rubs, Roderick," she said coyly, cutting her blue eyes to look up at him.

Felicia felt her stomach turn over.

"I won't be long," Roderick said, the businesslike voice he had used with Felicia draining into more dulcet tones.

Roderick set up the next day's schedule with Felicia and Juan Carlos before he and the model left. Felicia made some excuse to stay behind until they were well out of sight. She didn't know how long her lunch would stay down if she had to watch Cheryl fawning all over Roderick on the way down in the elevator.

The next day was no better. Felicia longed for her duties on this assignment to end. Soon Roderick Bearstern would surely realize he was wasting her time and his. She would never model for him, and no amount of exposure to the glamorous life of a top model was going to change her mind. In spite of how desperately she wanted money for her mother's care, she knew modeling was not the way to earn it.

That afternoon, at the end of the session, Roderick announced he was taking the entire crew out to dinner at one of Barcelona's most famous restaurants. "I insist that everyone be there," he ordered, his brown eyes settling on Felicia with a meaningful glitter. She chuckled to herself wryly. This was one command she felt no compunction about disobeying. She might be obligated to Roderick during the day as his translator, but nothing in her agreement with his company spelled out having to spend her free evenings in his presence. She felt absolutely smug about the prospect of having an opportunity to defy the arrogant Mr. Bearstern.

But Felicia Farr had not reckoned with the persistence of her adversary. For that night, just as Felicia was about to settle down with a good book for an hour or two before the customary late dinner in Spain, she heard a knock at her door.

"Who is it?" she called out in Spanish. While a few of her friends from her years here knew she was back in the country, she was not expecting anybody.

The knock was harder and more insistent the second time.

"Felicia!" a familiar voice rasped. "Open this door."

An invisible hand squeezed Felicia's heart at the sound of Roderick Bearstern's voice. She momentarily thought she might smother from the sudden constriction.

She rose from the bed and headed for the door. Her fingers shook as she reached out to open the lock.

"Just as I thought!" Roderick snapped, when the dim light from the hall fell across her robed body. "You weren't coming tonight, were you?"

"Well, I—I . . ." Felicia stammered, her pounding heart sending a rush of blood to her head that confused her.

Roderick brushed past her, made a quick survey of the room, strode over to the overstuffed chair beside the bed and sat down, folding his arms across his chest. She felt his brown eyes rake down her body, scowling at the formless chenille bathrobe tied at the waist with a limp sash.

"Get dressed!" he ordered.

"No!" she shot back, her courage returning. "I don't have to accept your dinner invitation."

"It was not an invitation," Roderick pointed out. "It was a directive. As long as you're working for me, you'll do as I tell you."

"Not on my own time," she countered haughtily

"Miss Felicia Farr," Roderick said angrily, rising from his chair and stalking her. "You have no free time on this assignment unless I give it to you. I'm paying you an excellent salary, and your commitment to me includes dinner parties if I so decide. I'm not leaving this room until you leave with me, if it takes all night."

Felicia stood spellbound at the overpowering presence of Roderick. He towered over her and made her feel weak and helpless. But the most frightening thing was the glimmer that leaped to his eyes when he threatened to spend the night, if necessary.

"You'd like that, wouldn't you?" Felicia gasped. "And you're just mean enough to do it."

"*Mean* is hardly the word I'd choose," Roderick said, a glow of satisfaction spreading across his face. He knew he'd won, Felicia realized. "I would say *determined* is more accurate."

"Call it what you like, the result is the same. You get your way," Felicia said caustically.

"Yes," Roderick agreed smugly. "And that's exactly the way I like it."

Hot anger, like molten lava, bubbled up in Felicia, but she had no options open to her. Like it or not, she had become a hostage of Roderick Bearstern while she was in Spain, and she knew it. She flounced over to the closet, grabbed a dress from the rack and slammed the bathroom door behind her.

The restaurant was magnificent. Had Felicia been dining here under any other circumstances, she would have loved it. But sitting to the right of Roderick while Cheryl sat on his left spoiled the magic atmosphere. Felicia hardly noticed the lingering scent of garlic and onion wafting from the plates of steaming food carried past their table by waiters in matador costumes. She barely heard the chattering of the rest of the crew seated around the massive table in the middle of the ornate room, which boasted beautiful paintings of rustic Spanish scenes. The Gothic architecture, with its archways and columns intermingled with angels and urns in relief on the walls, transported the diners to a time past, which set the proper mood for the old, authentic Spanish food on the menu.

Instead of each individual placing a separate order, the patrons selected a few special dishes cooked in quantity and served family style. In spite of her anger, Felicia was hungry, and she spent her time listening to the Spanish orchestra play soft, melodious tunes and wishing the food would arrive soon.

"We might as well dance while we're waiting for dinner," Roderick said to the crew. Heads turned in his direction, nodded in assent, and couples began forming out of the circle of people seated randomly around the table.

Cheryl leaned close to Roderick and batted her eyelashes at him, a gesture Felicia read as an expectation that he would ask the model to dance with him. Instead, Juan Carlos approached, held out his hand with a continental sweep and bowed from the waist.

"Go ahead," Roderick urged her. "He wants to dance with you."

"But, Roderick," Cheryl protested, clutching his arm and pressing her ample bosom against his wrist.

"Go on," Roderick insisted. "Don't insult the man."

Cheryl pushed out her bottom lip, shot Felicia a murderous glance and followed Juan Carlos out onto the dance floor.

It was with a nervous clearing of her throat that Felicia inadvertently called Roderick's attention to the fact that she and he were the final diners left at the now empty table. She didn't relish the thought of sitting with him alone, but even worse was the prospect of having to dance with him . . . to be held close in his powerful arms, to feel his warm breath caress her cheek in an intimate embrace.

"Excuse me," she said softly, picking up her purse and rising from her chair. "Which way to the ladies' room?" He had turned his brown eyes on her, and she had reacted with the first thought that came into her mind.

"That can wait," Roderick said brusquely, seizing her by the wrist and extracting the purse from her fist. "You don't need to do any primping. You look fine."

"B-but . . ." she protested in vain.

"Come on," he insisted. "I want to talk to you, in private. We can do that best on the dance floor."

Before she could marshall the inner resources to resist, Roderick had led her out to the swaying couples, and he had encircled her with his muscular arms. He pressed her supple body against his firm physique and put his right hand on the small of her back, pulling her in close to him. She felt her soft flesh yield to his firm muscles, and she was surprised at how well her frame melted against his, especially considering how tall he was.

Her breath caught in her throat when Roderick nestled his face in her hair. His warm breath stirring her hair and settling on her bare shoulders sent an involuntary shudder through her. She wondered if he could feel her heart thumping wildly in her chest. Her palms began to perspire. Roderick was so close, they moved as one entity across the dance floor, and the rivulet of breeze their bodies created as they passed through the air left behind the lingering masculine scent of Roderick's after shave lotion for others to enjoy. For some reason she didn't understand, Felicia begrudged losing even that small a part of the wholeness of Roderick Bearstern. She had fallen under his spell, a magic strength of possession that enveloped her with its power and made her want to cling to this moment and this feeling forever. While she hated Roderick and everything he stood for, she could not escape the undeniable truth that he exuded an irresistible appeal even she was victim to. Maybe it was a dangerous game, allowing herself to enjoy the closeness of this man, permitting herself to give in to the heavenliness of the moment, letting herself close her eyes and dance among the clouds in a dream world, where it was all right to flow with the sensual mood Roderick was creating in her. Never before had a man stirred her longings so, kindled such a flame of desire in her. Could it be so wrong to enjoy the moment for what it was—a one time rapture of being held by a man with the animal magnetism women dream about? After all, she hated Roderick Bearstern. So it was all right to let him turn all her senses on fire, because they both knew this moment was only a physical attraction, a mixing of two body chemistries that produced hot flashes of burning desire that would lead to absolutely nothing.

Felicia opened her eyes, and a jolt of reality burned shamefully through her. What was she thinking? Here she was in Roderick Bearstern's arms, daydreaming like some dewey-eyed teenager about romance under the stars. What kind of evil man was he, anyway, to be able to cast such a spell over her? She detested the man, and what she had been feeling in his arms was scandalous.

"The music's stopped," she pointed out, wrestling herself from his arms, her cheeks burning with the knowledge of her sensual desire for this man.

She turned to retreat to the safety of the dining table, but Roderick grabbed her wrist and pulled her back to him. "I haven't told you why I wanted to talk to you, yet," he said. "We'll dance again."

"You had your chance during an entire tune," she said. "Besides, Cheryl's coming this way with Juan Carlos, and she has a determined look in her eyes."

"Never mind her," Roderick said, without so much as a glance in her direction. The orchestra began playing the next tune, and Roderick whisked Felicia past the furious model, who stood with her eyes blazing hot coals of hate at the two of them. "I didn't tell you what I had on my mind because you were obviously enjoying yourself so much I didn't want to break into your thoughts. Have you found out that I'm not so bad after all? Most women find me irresistible," he said with an arrogant grin.

Felicia's face glowed with embarrassment. Had Roderick suspected what she was thinking? What a conceited man he was!

"I find you pompously stuck on yourself!" Felicia sniffed disdainfully. "A quality which hardly lends anything to your lack of charm, Mr. Bearstern."

"Thank you," Roderick said with a hearty laugh. "I knew I could sweep you off your feet."

Ignoring his sarcasm, Felicia said, "Just what did you want to talk to me about?"

"About a little favor I plan to do for you."

"A favor?" Felicia asked. The only thing she wanted from him was to be released from her current duties. Was he actually going to grant her wish?

"Yes," Roderick said, turning serious. "I know all about your mother and how she has refused to see you, and I'm going to help you break down her defenses."

"How?" Felicia gasped. All at once, she completely forgot about Roderick's position and who he was. For the moment he was simply a compelling, dynamic man offering to help her, and Felicia's distrust of him withered away with the prospect of his help.

"By using the one surefire method that will gain her attention and ensure that she will see you."

"Which is?" Felicia inquired eagerly.

Just then, the music stopped again, and Roderick held her long after the last note had vibrated into silence. This time Felicia didn't pull herself away from Roderick. She turned her long-lashed, deep blue eyes up to meet his gaze, and the flicker of green in his brown orbs spoke to her of desire and compassion. The blood rushed past her eardrums so furiously that she failed to hear the band start up again, and she moved, as if in a dream, with Roderick's body, swaying, not to the music of the band, but to the rhythm of Roderick's hard, muscular body. Her body flowed against his, and his eyes caressed her face and neck. Goose bumps popped out on her arms and back. Sounds of the band's playing began to penetrate her senses, and she felt as if she and Roderick were two people alone in the world, wrapped in a cocoon of soft music intended for them and them alone. The drums pounded in rhythm with the beating of her heart, and the trumpet sang of two hearts entwined in rapture. His possessive hands gripped her, and she melted in willing submission.

"A sure way to break down your mother's resistance is to send her a photograph of you," Roderick said. "I'll have Juan Carlos shoot it tomorrow."

For a moment the full ramification of Roderick's words failed to penetrate Felicia's dream world. But as her mind digested his statement, her perception of her surroundings underwent a drastic alteration. The soft, warm glow of shadowy lights that a few moments before had whispered of love and romance now bespoke a sinister plot directed at her. The compassionate expression in Roderick's eyes turned into a murky deception hidden behind unspoken conspiracies against her.

She stiffened in his arms, her knees locking into place.

"You never give up, do you?" she demanded angrily. "That's absolutely disgusting. Using a phony concern for my problem with my mother to get me in front of your cameras!"

"It's not phony, Felicia," Roderick insisted. "Besides, what do you care about my motivations? If I can help you get your mother to see you, what difference does it make how I do it?"

"Just how did you find out about my mother, anyway?" Felicia demanded, mechanically responding to Roderick's lead as he directed her around the dance floor to a slow waltz. "I didn't tell you she wouldn't see me. Have you had your spies at work again?"

"It wasn't all that difficult, really." Roderick shrugged. "One of my detectives found a nurse only too eager to talk for the right amount of money. That kind of information is confidential, but most people have a price. . . ."

"So you figured to have the goods just in case I wasn't willing to pose for you after you tricked me into working for you, is that it?" Felicia snapped. "Roderick Bearstern, you have absolutely no principles!"

"Think what you like, Felicia," Roderick said with a touch of bitterness ringing in his words. "But if you're sensible, you'll realize what a favor I'm doing you. How long has it been since you've had a decent photograph taken of yourself? Have you considered how your mother will feel when she receives a picture of her only daughter, smiling out at her, pleading with her to see you? What mother could resist that?"

"No, I won't do it!" Felicia argued adamantly.

"And pass up the chance of a lifetime? Your mother may never come around to wanting to see you, Felicia. The nurse said Francine's hiding behind a cloak of shame and guilt for the way she treated you. But you can penetrate that protective shell. Once your mother sees a picture of you, she'll be jolted out of the imaginary world she's built for you. She'll realize you're a real flesh-and-blood person, not just a hand-written name at the end of a letter. You'll become real to her. You'll take on a shape, a definite appearance in her mind, and she'll feel compelled to see you. It will work, Felicia, believe me, it will."

"And why should I believe you?" Felicia said through tautly drawn lips. "You haven't told me the truth about anything yet."

"Because you know I'm right," Roderick said with a confidence that disturbed Felicia. "If you don't do this, then you also know I'm right about something else."

"What?"

"What I said before," Roderick reminded her. "You don't really want to see your mother and get to know her. Because if you do, you'll find out the truth, and you'll have to stop feeling sorry for yourself."

Roderick's words were like a slap in the face. A tingle shot through Felicia, and she wondered if there were some truth in what he said. She was too emotionally involved to tackle this problem intellectually. She would have to work it out in her own heart.

While her mother had refused to see her, Felicia had never pushed her way past her mother's objections. She supposed she could have physically intruded on her mother, demanding to see her, refusing to take no for an answer. At the time, she had told herself, she had used self-restraint for the sake of her mother's condition. But had that been the real reason? Had she actually been afraid to confront her mother? Her thoughts tumbled over each other in a labyrinth of confusion, and suddenly she felt tired.

"We'll take the photographs tomorrow," Roderick said.

It was a dirty blow, Felicia thought. He had sensed a moment of vulnerability, and he had attacked her weakened emotions at the fatal instant.

"No!" she fumed, stalking off the floor in the direction of the table. But the word had a hollow ring, and she knew Roderick had heard the echo that belied her exclamation.

Chapter Five

"This way, Miss Farr," said the makeup girl who wore a touch too much rouge but looked glowing in spite of it.

Felicia had arrived at the studio early, still undecided about whether or not to go through with this venture. She changed her mind once, took a taxi almost all the way back to her hotel, and then directed the driver to return her to the studio.

Roderick was trying to manipulate her, she knew. But she wasn't going into this deal with her eyes closed. She wasn't so naive that she didn't understand his motivation. He was willing to try any trick to get her in front of the camera. She was hesitant to play into his hands. But the truth of what he had said had not escaped her. A photograph of herself might be just the key to unlock her mother's exile, and she was willing to try almost anything.

Felicia was led into the dressing room at the left of

the main office, and she found herself surrounded by an entourage of assistants. Consternation pleated her brow in little furrows as she realized what was going on.

"Wait a minute," she protested. "I'm not here to be made over. I'm just going to have a simple photograph taken."

"But you do want to look your best," said an older woman, who directed Felicia to a beauty-shop chair in front of a large sink.

"Well, that's true. . . ." Felicia conceded.

Before she could protest further, Felicia was seated in the chair and reclined over the sink. Warm water splashed on her hair and scalp.

Well, she mumbled silently to herself, she couldn't have her photograph taken with wet hair, so she might as well let them proceed. The rosy aroma of an expensive shampoo wafted past her nostrils, and Felicia began to relax and feel drowsy under the skillful fingers massaging her scalp. She was accustomed to washing her own hair, so it was a soothing sensation to have disembodied hands caressing her head.

Just then, the makeup girl touched Felicia's cheek, and Felicia's fuzzy vision cleared. "What are you doing?" she demanded, startled by the unexpected encounter.

"Just trying to pick the appropriate makeup base," the girl said pleasantly.

"I don't need that," Felicia said.

"But Mr. Bearstern gave me orders. . . ." the girl said.

"Oh, he did, did he?" Felicia said knowingly. So he was trying to trick her. Well, it would do him no good. Felicia knew Roderick could neither sell nor publish her photographs without a model release. And she would never sign one. So he could doll her up all he wanted to, take as many shots of her as he wished, but the photos would be useless to him. If he refused to let her have copies to send her mother, she would just wait until she returned to the States and could afford to have the pictures retaken at a local photo studio.

"Okay," Felicia conceded. "But make it simple. I don't go in for heavy makeup."

The makeup girl smiled and began to dab at Felicia's face and smooth lotions on her skin. While the older woman blew her hair dry, Felicia allowed the younger girl to apply a touch of mascara to her long eyelashes. Then her hands were gently lifted and placed in a bowl of liquid, and she watched as she was given a manicure.

The finishing touches were applied with little brushes of color on her cheeks. The older woman pulled a soft-bristled brush through Felicia's hair and arranged puffy layers of her tresses over her shoulders. She shot a film of hair spray at her from behind and above, and spun the chair to face the room, so that Felicia could stand.

Next she was handed a red silk dress that slipped cooly over her skin as the makeup girl helped her change so that she didn't disturb her beauty treatment. The girl cinched the belt snugly around Felicia's small waist and straightened the hem that draped gracefully around her well-shaped calves.

"Now, let's have a look at you," the older woman suggested, as she took Felicia by the hand and led her to a full-length mirror at the far end of the room.

Felicia gasped at her reflection. She was too stunned to speak.

"She looks gorgeous," the makeup girl observed.

"Yes," the older woman agreed. "You did wonders with her face. She really does look like those old photos."

"The trick is with the mascara," the makeup girl said. "I feathered her lashes toward the outer corners for a sultry effect. It goes well with her wide-eyed innocent look."

"Mr. Bearstern should be pleased," the older woman mused, eyeing Felicia's reflection.

Felicia stood immobile. While there were differences in her appearance from her mother's old photographs, Felicia was shocked at how much she truly resembled her mother.

Just then, she heard a long, low whistle, and she looked into the mirror to see Roderick staring at her over her shoulder.

"You look sensational!" he said, his brown eyes devouring her twice, once in person and again in the mirror.

Felicia whirled and confronted him, her eyes brimming with hot tears. "What are you trying to do to me?" she demanded.

"Nothing," Roderick said reassuringly, "but take your picture just as I said."

"You didn't have to do this," she fumed, "just to photograph me for my mother. You're trying to make me over. You're determined to revive my mother's image, and if I won't cooperate with you, you'll stoop to any trick to try to force me!"

"What are you afraid of, Felicia?" Roderick asked, taking her by the hand and leading her from the dressing room.

Felicia's flesh burned where Roderick touched her, and she tried to wrest her arm free of his grasp. But he held her firmly.

"I'm not afraid of anything," Felicia retorted.

"Then let's get on with it," Roderick ordered, as he pulled her into the studio and led her toward the pale pink backdrop in front of the camera.

"No!" Felicia protested, ignoring Juan Carlos as he fiddled with the equipment. Her entire attention was riveted on Roderick Bearstern, and she failed to hear the snap of a camera being readied for action.

"You've come too far to back out now," Roderick

said forcefully. "I'm not going to let you pass up this chance to break through your mother's defenses against you."

"What difference does my relationship with my mother make to you?" Felicia demanded.

"Plenty," Roderick said with an undercurrent of emotion that puzzled Felicia.

Then a flash of insight struck her. "Oh, I get it," she said stiffly. "If Mother agrees to see me, you think that will somehow change my mind about letting you use me for your Francine Farr revival."

"Go ahead and shoot, Juan Carlos," Roderick said. "She's not going to cooperate, so we'll do what we can under the circumstances."

Suddenly Felicia's body stiffened. For what seemed like a full minute, while the camera was clicking rapidly, she stood immobile. Waves of different expressions crossed her face as she sorted through her emotions for the appropriate response. She was sure her ears had not played tricks on her. And yet, the two languages were so familiar to her, she didn't even bother to shift mental gears when she switched from one to the other. But in spite of the natural sound of both languages to her, she finally realized that Roderick had spoken to Juan Carlos in flawless Spanish.

"Roderick Bearstern, your little game is up!" Felicia snapped. "You brought me here under totally false pretexts, lied to me and tried to trick me, and unmercifully played on my feelings about my mother. You didn't need an interpreter. You speak perfect Spanish!"

"Of course." Roderick nodded casually. "Surely you must have known I could hardly conduct my business here in Spain until you arrived if I hadn't spoken Spanish. Underneath all that external blustering, you really want to play into my hands. But you can't bring yourself to admit it. So I've put you in a position where you can give in and still keep your conscience intact."

"And just where did you get your degree in psychology?" Felicia demanded coldly. "Has it never occurred to you that I might be telling the truth about my feelings?"

"Certainly," Roderick said condescendingly, taking a step toward her. "You are telling the truth, as you believe you know it. But I've been around a lot of women, Felicia," he said, his brown eyes glittering with a strange expression. "And I know more about you than you do. You're confused right now. You think you hate modeling because it robbed you of your mother. You're bitter toward her, but at the same time you want to help her so you can get to know her. Right now, you're experiencing a love-hate relationship that has you so rattled, you don't know what you want."

A spark shot through Felicia as her gaze lay captured by Roderick's stare. Was he touching sensitive nerves with his armchair analysis? Or was it his nearness that made her hair prickle. No, no, it couldn't be that. She wouldn't allow it to be that. It was his ridiculous assumptions that had her so upset. Personally he had no effect on her, except to stir up her anger.

"Oh!" Felicia exploded. She shot Roderick a deadly look and stormed off the set, choking back tears she was determined not to let him see. Her emotions were ravaged into tatters she felt she would never be able to sew back together in the proper order.

In the dressing room, Felicia splashed cold water on her face at the sink, found a jar of cold cream and angrily smeared its contents on her cheeks and chin, and tissued the residue away. She rubbed as hard as she could, enjoying the sting as her flesh grew pink under the assault.

She deserved to hurt, she thought miserably. Anyone stupid enough to be taken in by Roderick Bearstern ought to suffer for such lack of intelligence. He had made a fool of her, feigning not to speak Spanish, and everyone involved must have been in on his little secret except Felicia. How they must have all laughed behind her back!

She hated Roderick for what he had done to her. But she hated him even more for the evil influence he had over her. Why did her heart race when she was near him? What a dirty trick life had played on her, matching up her emotional chemistry with a man she would despise until the day she died!

Felicia slipped out of the red silk dress and into her own ordinary clothes. When she fled the studio, no one tried to stop her. She went directly to her hotel, took out her suitcases and furiously tossed her clothes into them. She slammed the lids with a bang, snapped the latches and flung them near the door. She stood there looking at them, realizing with a pang that she wasn't going anywhere until Roderick Bearstern provided the wherewithall. With that, she flung herself on the bed and cried bitter tears of anger and frustration.

The next morning, Felicia awoke from a fitful night of troubled sleep. She had spent the rest of the previous day trying to sort out her feelings. But she seemed no closer at all to understanding the whirlpool that was pulling her into its vortex. Her life had taken a sudden change of late, and she couldn't figure out how to get back on solid terrain, with people she understood and activities that made sense to her.

Just as Felicia was about to leave her room to go to the hotel coffee shop for breakfast, the phone rang. It was probably Roderick, she realized glumly. Well, she wasn't going to answer. She started to walk out on the second jangle, but she had a sudden flash that stopped her. Suppose he was downstairs calling on the house phone? He would surely see her as soon as she emerged in the lobby. She would just wait out the call in her room and then decide whether to chance going downstairs.

Roderick was too clever not to know that she was forced to eat her meals in the hotel. He had provided her small amounts of spending money at first, but he had cut that off, and now she had to sign for her meals in the coffee shop so that they could be charged to her room. Roderick was not taking any chances of her skipping out on him. He made sure she was financially dependent on him while she was in Spain.

Felicia waited for several minutes after the phone stopped ringing. She paced the floor, nervously picking at the cuticles of her nails.

Suddenly a rapping at the door made her start. "Felicia," Roderick's voice called out. Her heart quickened. She froze to the spot. All she could hear was the rasping of her rapid, short breaths.

"Felicia?" Roderick's voice pierced the air again. A few more raps, and then all fell silent.

Felicia tiptoed to the door, placed her ear gingerly against the smooth wood and listened. She heard nothing. But dare she assume Roderick had actually departed? Maybe he suspected she was hiding from him and was waiting out in the hall, ready to confront her if she opened the door.

As quietly as possible, she made her way to the chair next to the bed and sat down. Every now and then, she heard footsteps pass her door, and each time, her pulse accelerated, but there was no further knocking.

Felicia glanced at her watch. It was midmorning, and she was beginning to feel definite pangs of hunger gnawing in the region of her stomach. As she sat there with the minutes ticking by, she grew increasingly aware of the futility of hiding out from Roderick. If it weren't for her desperate emotional need to see and get to know her mother, she would be sorely tempted to just stay in Spain. She could find a job here. She knew people who would help her. But nothing was going to keep her from doing everything she could to get her mother to see her, no matter what the cost. And that meant she was going to have to face Roderick sooner or later. She might as well get it over with, she thought grimly.

Felicia opened the door to her room, her heart pounding so hard it took her breath away. She looked up and down the hall. It was deserted, except for the maid. She lunched in the coffee shop with her eyes warily directed at the entrance, but Roderick was disturbingly absent. She returned to her room and locked herself in, still wrestling with the decision of whether or not to let him in if he returned. First she resolved to be done with the confrontation. Then she backed away from the idea. Back and forth, back and forth bounced her decision, until she earnestly wished he would return and she could put an end to this indecision. Facing Roderick wouldn't be nearly as stressful as not knowing what she was going to do.

When the knock finally came that afternoon, Felicia thought her heart would choke off her breath completely.

"Felicia, let me in," Roderick ordered between sharp raps on her door.

Felicia rubbed her clammy palms on her skirt. She swallowed hard before turning the latch and then backed away from the door as if its touch would burn her.

"It's open," she called in a thin voice.

The door swung in, and the dark, tall frame of Roderick Bearstern filled the opening. Felicia's heart picked up tempo. She didn't want to look at him, but she couldn't help noticing him before she turned her back on him. His hair was glistening from touches of a gentle mist she had not known was falling. Small beads of dew clung to his eyebrows and eyelashes, making him look like a seafarer home from a stormy adventure on the ocean. His brown eyes sparkled with a strange expression of anticipation that unnerved her. He wanted something from her, she sensed, and she hated herself for her traitorous impulse to give it to him, no matter what it was.

"I have the pictures," Roderick said. She turned, and he held out a manila envelope to her. "I think these will convince your mother to see you."

"But I didn't pose for you," Felicia protested.

"It doesn't matter," Roderick explained. "While you and I were arguing, Juan Carlos took a fast series of shots. Between scowls, you relaxed enough for him to get some good expressions. Your mother will never guess the circumstances under which these photographs were taken. You look lovely. Your face is animated."

Color rose to Felicia's cheeks. Roderick's tone was soft, warm, almost caressing. She was ashamed at how much she liked the sound of it. She was mortified that she cared what Roderick thought of her photographs, that he found them, and her, lovely.

Roderick sat down in the chair and pulled Felicia down to sit on the arm while he opened the envelope. Felicia's skin burned from his touch. Her mouth went dry and cottony. She heard a rushing sound of blood in her ears.

"Look," Roderick said. "What did I tell you?" He handed Felicia several prints. Her gaze bounced off the shiny paper, and the subject of the photo barely registered in her brain. It was impossible for her mind to absorb so many stimuli all at once, and the predominant message getting through to her conscious mind was the nearness of this man she hated. It was absolutely scandalous that he should affect her in this way. All she could concentrate on was the tingle she felt when she caught the scent of his manly aroma, the charge of excitement galloping through her as her gaze spilled over the top of the photos and took in the muscles of his thighs straining at the dark material of his trousers. She found herself unable to take her eyes off his large, well-shaped hands, with black hairs curling seductively on the back.

Felicia was so close to Roderick, she felt warm all over from his body heat. She had to get away from him, she realized. A warning bell sounded in her brain, and she rose from the chair and walked toward the window, pretending to look at the photos.

"Well?" Roderick asked expectantly. "Don't you think they're sensational?"

Felicia shook her head to clear the cobwebs from her vision and forced her eyes to look at the photos. She gasped. If any photograph she had ever had taken would convince her mother to see her, these would surely do it. It wasn't until she saw herself on paper that Felicia realized the startling resemblance between herself and the glamorous pictures she had seen of her mother when Francine Farr was at the height of her fame.

True, Felicia had darker blond hair than her mother had had, and her eyebrows were arched differently, but there was no mistaking the family resemblance. Anyone could see that Felicia was Francine's daughter, or maybe even her sister.

She hated to admit it, but Roderick had been right to dress her up and glamorize her for these photos. What woman could resist seeing a daughter who looked almost exactly like her? Curiosity would eventually outweigh her feelings of guilt and remorse, and Francine would agree to let Felicia visit her. At least she hoped so.

But how could Felicia show Roderick her gratitude? She had accused him of trickery, and maybe trickery it was. Perhaps he would try to turn her gratitude into defeat. She was not about to sign a model release, so he needn't try that route. She wasn't going to go to work for him, so just what was his motivation?

The words *thank you* stuck in Felicia's throat. Would she be making a fool of herself again to say them? The best she could manage was a question. "Why did you do this for me?" she asked warily.

The glimmer in Roderick's brown eyes dimmed. His lids drooped. Silently, he stood up, strode over to the window and stood beside Felicia.

Her heart speeded up. Only now did she become aware of the dampness in the room seeping in around the windowpane. Only now did she see the trickles of mist gleaming like watery diamonds running down the glass that Roderick looked through to the outside city of Barcelona. He had a faraway, troubled expression in his eyes.

"Because I know how you feel," he said. "And I wanted to help you."

"What do you mean?" Felicia asked, her anger melting away into a pool of empathy for a man who somehow evoked a storm of emotions in her that she knew paralleled a similar response in him. It was as if, for the first time, he was venting a genuine emotion that she could relate to, and she suddenly felt very close to him.

"Let's just say I've been in your shoes, too," Roderick said, his voice thick with emotion.

Involuntarily, Felicia reached out and touched Roderick's hand. His eyes darted toward her fingers, and then he lifted his lids so that he was staring right into her eyes.

Felicia's breath caught in her chest. Roderick's expression changed from stony and cold to vulnerable and soft. "Tell me about it," she heard herself say.

A curious, fleeting frown swept over Roderick's face. Then he tilted his head to one side almost imperceptibly and asked, "You mean you're interested?" he murmured, as if carefully measuring her reaction.

"Of course," she tried to answer impersonally, but even *she* heard the depth of emotion carried in the tone of her voice.

"I've never told anyone how I feel about this," Roderick said slowly, his eyes reading Felicia's face for any sign of mockery.

"If anyone would understand, I would," Felicia reassured him. "After all, you said it's something akin to my experience."

Roderick looked at her a long time, his eyes probing hers, and she realized he was searching her soul for the kind of understanding he probably had felt no one would ever be able to offer him. He obviously held some secret locked in his heart, and he had never planned to reveal it to anyone. But circumstances, coupled with a kindred soul, had pushed him to the brink of revelation, and he was proceeding with extreme caution.

"I never knew my mother, either," Roderick said. His bitter tone revealed how deeply he had been hurt by what he was telling Felicia. She had heard the same tone of voice many times before, when she had talked about her mother.

"My situation was somewhat different from yours," he went on. "My mother was around physically. But she might as well have been in a foreign country, or on the moon for that matter. She hid in a bottle. She was an alcoholic when my father married her, but he didn't know it. She was very clever at hiding the alcoholic episodes until after the wedding. My father tried to get help for her, but she wouldn't cooperate. Oh, she'd promise to reform from time to time in order to wheedle expensive presents from my father or to get him to buy her some new clothes to wear for her 'reformation.' But it never lasted more than a day or two."

"You mean she's still drinking?" Felicia asked, a wave of sympathy sweeping over her.

"Not anymore," Roderick said sadly. "She drank herself to death. I never had a chance to get to know the real woman drowned under all that booze. I tried my best to get her to stop drinking for my sake, but she was too addicted to care how her alcoholism affected me. All she could think about was that bottle. My father loved her deeply in the beginning. But as the years wore on, he lost both his love and his respect for her. He fell in love with someone else, but he had too much regard for the institution of marriage to do anything about it."

"What about after your mother died?"

"I don't know. My father never talked about it very much. He just said the situation was impossible. He never even told me who the woman was."

"And so you felt you were cheated out of having a mother?" Felicia asked, tears springing to her eyes at her own pain and for the suffering Roderick had experienced.

"Yes," Roderick said huskily, "so I knew just how you felt about your mother. I wanted to help you. My chance to know my mother is gone forever, but yours is not. These photos may be just the thing to turn her thinking in your favor."

"Yes," Felicia said hopefully. "They might do it. Thank you, Roderick." She looked up into his eyes, and she felt an electric charge jump between them. It was as if a magic spell had been cast over them, and they were suddenly of one mind and of one spirit. A river of understanding flowed between them, and it drew them closer and closer together, like a forceful tide pushing two willing vessels prow to prow.

Silently, Roderick reached out his arms and embraced Felicia. The photographs dropped from her hands and fluttered to the floor. The cool rivulets of breeze bouncing off the windowpane encircled a man and a woman in each other's arms and provided a buffer between them and reality. For now, they were in their own world, just the two of them, bound together by a common bond of understanding and past hurt that melded certain portions of their deeper feelings into a single unit suspended in time and space.

Roderick stared down at Felicia, his large brown eyes seeming to consume the totality of her being. She felt her consciousness being absorbed into his as he held her soft, curvaceous body tightly against the hard muscular plane of his physique.

Roderick lifted one hand and slowly trailed his index finger along the outline of Felicia's upper lip. A shudder of desire passed through her, warming her skin and causing her breath to come in sudden jerks. Her muscles grew fluid, and she melted against Roderick, a willing prisoner of his arms. Her face tilted upward as his finger found the soft, velvet flesh of her mouth and tempted her with a feathery touch that sent a sprinkling tingle racing along her spine.

Felicia felt herself hypnotized as Roderick continued his sensual caressing, now touching her cheeks lightly with the tips of his fingers, hinting of the promise of fulfillment in his arms. A deep animal longing was growing inside her, and she pressed herself eagerly against Roderick, silently begging him with her half-closed eyes to go on. She was being lulled into a rapturous cocoon of wanton desire, and she craved the experience waiting at the crest of the next plateau, and the next, and the next, until she reached the summit of some emotional and physical peak that she only now vaguely understood.

Just before she cried out for Roderick to sweep her

along with the stormy swells of her emotion, he broke the moorings that had held her at abeyance. He closed his eyes, tilted his head toward her and captured her mouth with his lips.

A spasm shook Felicia, and she thought her body would burst from the sheer ecstasy of Roderick's kiss. His mouth drew from hers all the intensity of feeling she had ever experienced. Her whole body grew warm and hungry for something she couldn't define. It was as if the creator had designed her with a flaw, a void of some kind that had lain dormant until now, and Roderick had been destined to fill that void. He had something she needed desperately, and she felt compelled to draw it from him, to satisfy a basic craving she had not realized existed in her.

She worked her mouth on his, frantic to extinguish the flame burning in her. But his nearness, the warmth of his breath, the touch of his flesh against hers, the manly aroma of his being, fanned the flame even higher. She felt a bewildering sense of unfulfillment coupled with an even stronger desire for satisfaction.

Felicia wrapped her arms around Roderick's neck, crushing her body against his. She pressed her lips even harder against his mouth, as if the sweet nectar of his kiss, if she could just wring enough of it from him, would cause her raging desire to abate.

Her entire body grew tense with excitement, and a pounding in her ears grew louder and louder until she thought she might faint from its intensity. The tension sapped all her strength, and when Roderick began to run his hand across the back of her neck, she went limp in his arms.

She stood motionless and ready as Roderick slowly slid his hands down her bare arms. Goose bumps of desire and anticipation popped out on her skin, and some of her muscles involuntarily flexed in spasms of desire and need.

Felicia lost all sense of time and place. The hotel room faded into a cloud of blurred colors revolving around two bodies exploring each other for the first time. All that was important at this moment was the gnawing hunger screaming out for satiation of the desire that Roderick had stirred up in Felicia. She didn't care what had happened before today or what would happen tomorrow. She was consumed with a passion like none she had ever experienced before in her life, and she was willing to go to any lengths to give vent to wherever that passion led her. Her body, her whole being, the entire spectrum of everything and anything that was Felicia Farr had been swept to a fever pitch of raw emotion that she could no longer control. Her one objective was to gain release from the wracking sensations that demanded fulfillment.

When Roderick lifted his mouth from hers, Felicia kept her eyes closed, her body and emotions ready for his next move. She knew now what her aching body was telling her, and she gladly waited for the touch of Roderick's hands on more intimate parts of her body.

But instead, she felt nothing. Slowly, she opened her eyes, and she found Roderick staring at her, his mouth red from their kiss, his expression puzzled, almost troubled. He, too, was breathing hard, his nostrils slightly flared, his pupils large black disks in his brown eyes.

"What's wrong?" she asked, anxiety twittering through her.

"I was about to take advantage of you," Roderick said thickly.

Well, go on, her mind screamed. But his words sent a chill of embarrassment through her, and she fought down the pulsating flames of desire that still licked at her. "How noble of you to stop," she said tartly, her words reflecting her bitter feeling of rejection.

"I better leave . . . while I'm still in control," Roderick said slowly, running his hand through his dark hair in an attempt to regain his composure.

"Yes. I wouldn't want you to do anything you'd regret in the morning," Felicia said caustically. The throbbing ache had lost some of its cutting edge, but Felicia realized it would take a long time for the full impact of it to ebb away.

Why had Roderick done this to her, she wondered. Was he deliberately showing her how much influence he had over her? Here she was in Spain, financially at his mercy, dependent on him for her very sustenance. Was he trying to demonstrate that she was at his mercy in other ways, too?

"Felicia," he said, as he walked slowly toward the door, apparently in some kind of discomfort, "I still want you to model for me. Now more than ever."

"More than ever?" she asked. "Why?" Her head was still reeling, but she detected an undercurrent of intensity that was different from his former brand of determination.

He paused, looked around the room quickly and then moved back near the window. He picked up the dropped photographs and held them out to her.

"Because of these," he said. "I've looked at them carefully. Your features photograph beautifully. Take a look, a good look, and see for yourself. You have great potential, Felicia. I'm not going to let you slip through my fingers."

A volcano of anger spewed up in Felicia. How could he have kissed her the way he did? He had told her one of the secrets of his soul, she had understood, and that experience had brought them so close together that she was willing—no eager—to give herself completely to him. But the whole thing had meant nothing to him. It was just a fleeting passionate embrace that was so trivial to him, he had stopped in the middle. How could something that had rocked Felicia to her very foundations have held so little significance for Roderick? How dare he stir up her passions to the highest peak of her desire and then reject her so coldly. What kind of hardhearted heel was he, anyway?

"You just did, Roderick," she said icily. "If I wasn't positive before, I'm dead sure now. Nothing on heaven or earth could ever convince me to model for you . . . under *any* circumstances."

"I'm sorry about what just happened, Felicia," Roderick apologized.

"Well, I'm not," Felicia retorted. "It showed me what kind of person you really are. And you're worse than I thought."

"You'll change your mind, Felicia," Roderick said knowingly. "I don't give up easily. You ought to know that by now."

"Your threats don't scare me," Felicia said, her voice quavering with emotion.

"It's not a threat, Felicia," Roderick said in a controlled monotone. "It's a promise." With that, he opened the door, filled the exit with his large frame and disappeared into the corridor.

Felicia marched to the open door, grabbed the knob and felt a measure of angry satisfaction when it slammed shut with a loud *clap!* Then she made a dash for the bed, threw herself across it and let loose a torrent of tears that trickled down her hands as she tried in vain to wipe the moisture from her cheeks.

What a hideous turn of events! She hated Roderick Bearstern with every fiber of her being. He had turned her into a simpering, loose woman, ready to give herself to him in exchange for one kiss.

And then, to top it all off, he had apologized for kissing her, as if he had regretted the whole thing! It had merely been a ruse, a clever trap to stir up her emotions so he could con her into posing for him for his great Francine Farr revival.

How she despised that man. He was nothing like Don. Don was sweet, likable, easygoing, just a big overgrown kid. Everyone liked him. Roderick, on the other hand, stirred up strong emotions in people, just as Juan Carlos had said.

Felicia thought of the many dates she and Don had had. They had both felt relaxed and comfortable with each other. No sparks flew when they got together. They had fallen into a predictable pattern, and their evenings together blurred into a bland routine, she realized with a twinge that made her feel just a little uncomfortable.

It disturbed her to think how different were her feelings toward Roderick Bearstern. There was certainly nothing dull about him or about their encounters. But she reminded herself that physical appeal meant nothing in the long run. And that was all he held for her, after all. She certainly couldn't stand the man's personality or character. He was commanding, dictatorial, egotistical. He believed in controlling his women and in taking charge of situations.

On the other hand, Felicia couldn't help remembering the look of pain in Roderick's eyes when he spoke of his mother. Under his stern exterior, he was quite sensitive. It was an emotion to which she could respond. After all, she had experienced the same thing he had. And she had been left feeling bitter and rejected, just as Roderick had.

Felicia realized that conflicting emotions about Roderick were weaving themselves around her thoughts in a crisscross pattern that was bewildering and confusing. Something inside her was being stirred up and marching inexorably in a direction that disturbed her.

In an attempt to control her loosed feelings, Felicia forced herself to think of Don, to picture his face in her mind, to concentrate on the kind of life she would lead if their relationship blossomed into full bloom. But thoughts of Roderick kept intruding in her mind. Try as she might, she couldn't will away the dark hair and eyes of a man who had swept her to the heights of ecstasy with one lingering kiss.

She wrestled willfully with those unwelcome thoughts of Roderick. A little voice was whispering truths about herself she didn't want to hear, and she tried to shame the voice into silence. But it persisted and haunted her and kept badgering her with its pronouncements until Felicia burst into a flood of fresh tears. *No!* her mind screamed at the voice. *No!* But she could no longer deny it. And slowly, ever so slowly, her conscious mind was forced to accept what her subconscious mind had known for a long time.

She could never be happy with a man like Don. Some women might be content with a three-bedroom house in the suburbs, two kids, a dog and a husband who came home from work every evening at five o'clock. But she would be bored to death. She needed a certain excitement and vibrancy in her life, and it was with a rush of tears that she realized the one man in the world who could make her truly happy was a man she had grown to despise. Somehow Roderick had turned her hate for him into the deepest, deadliest kind of love, and she knew that no matter how long she lived or how many men she met, she would never love anyone except Roderick Bearstern.

Chapter Six

"I—I don't know how to tell you this, Don," Felicia said stiffly, her voice cracking with emotion.

Felicia had returned to the United States a few days ahead of Roderick, and she had the feeling the whole world had changed in her absence. Don looked younger, more boyish than ever. Her apartment seemed more cramped, as if the walls enjoyed confining her inside while she wallowed in her misery. She had let several days lapse before contacting Don, and even now, she was too ashamed to admit how long she had been back in the States.

Don sat on the couch, his blue eyes following her as she paced the room. His perplexed expression revealed that he knew something was amiss. But he waited patiently, listening quietly, while Felicia struggled to find the right words.

"I'll always think of you as a friend, Don. You've been wonderful to me. Almost like a brother."

"Friend? Brother?" Don asked, his voice fringed with disappointment. "Is that the furthest your feelings have gone for me?"

"It's so hard to explain," Felicia said, tears cresting on her lids.

"Something must have happened in Spain," Don said thoughtfully. "What was it? Can you tell me about it?"

Felicia looked at Don, sitting there on the couch, his sandy-colored hair and clean good looks so appealing to her. And yet, it was an appeal without the intensity she felt whenever she looked at Roderick. Don was like a big, lovable kid, like one of her boy students who had wormed his way into her heart, but who could never be more than just a friend. She felt miserable having to tell Don the truth about her feelings, but she couldn't string him along, letting him think their relationship could develop into something serious. But neither could she bear to say the words that would tell him what was in her heart.

"I don't know," she choked. "It's all so hard to understand. I'm not sure I myself know what happened. I just need time, Don. Time to sort through my own feelings. Time to figure out what I'm going to do, what I want out of life. Right now I can't handle any involvements, any pressure of any kind."

"Did you meet someone else while you were in Spain?" Don asked. "Some romantic Spaniard?"

"No," Felicia said tersely. "I'm immune to the flowery phrases of Latins. After all, I grew up over there. I know all their lines."

"Then what is it?" Don asked, his gaze penetrating Felicia's cloak of guilt. He reached out and took her hand in his, pulling her in his direction and down beside him on the couch.

Felicia wanted to withdraw her hand. She felt like a traitor letting one man hold her hand when her heart belonged to another. But she owed Don a certain amount of consideration. After all, she had left the United States with the understanding that she was his woman. And now, she was returning a few weeks later and telling him their relationship was all over—at least the romantic aspect of it.

"I don't know exactly," she hedged. She wasn't lying completely. The truth was she didn't know exactly how Roderick Bearstern had made her fall in love with him or what she was going to do about it. Nothing, probably. What could she do about it, except feel miserable? She wasn't going to run off and hide somewhere while she tried to heal her emotional wounds, not as long as her mother was hospitalized nearby and might consent to see her.

"It's all tied up with my mother," Felicia said at last. It was the only plausible explanation that might make a bit of sense to Don. "I had some photographs of myself taken and sent them to her. I think they may convince her to see me. I'm so uptight now, I can't concentrate on anything. I want to be alone for a time. I—I don't know, I'm just terribly confused, Don."

Felicia had never told Don about Roderick, and to do so now would seem like the worst kind of treachery. Strange, she realized. There was no real reason to keep the truth from Don. And yet in her heart, she knew it was a secret she must guard forever. No one must know how deeply and hopelessly she loved a man she should despise.

"I'm not sure I understand, Felicia," Don said at last. "But if that's how you feel, I can't argue with your emotions. I won't call you anymore until you decide you need me. When you do, all you have to do is pick up the phone. I'll be waiting to hear from you."

"Thank you, Don," Felicia said gratefully, squeezing

Don's hand with a genuine rush of affection. Maybe it was better this way, she thought. She could break up with him in stages. First she would ask for this time to herself, then later she would tell him that she could never be anything more than just a friend. It would be hard facing him at school next year, but she could be secure in the knowledge that she had not led him on when she knew it was all over between them.

She walked with Don to the door, and he pecked her gently on the mouth. Felicia let out a deep sigh when the door closed, and she stood feeling cold and empty, as if she had died inside. She had never realized love could make anyone feel so miserable. All the fairy tales of her childhood had ended with the hero and heroine getting married and living happily ever after. In spite of the warnings she had heard that life was not like a fairy tale, she had secretly harbored the belief that for her, it would be. She would meet her knight in shining armor, he would sweep her off her feet, and they would ride off into the sunset together in blissful happiness. That was how she had imagined love would be for her. Instead, she had met a man who turned her emotions to fire. She hated him almost as much as she loved him, and they would never resolve the differences that would keep them apart forever.

Felicia moped around her apartment for days, a lethargy of remorse and bitterness for what might have been choking off all desire to do anything. She knew she had to get a grip on herself, but right now she didn't have the will to force herself out of her melancholy mood. She ate little, watched a few mindless TV programs, and slept away much of her depression.

Finally, Felicia realized she couldn't waste the rest of her summer feeling sorry for herself. She still might be able to make a little money if she could get some assignments through one of the temporary employment agencies. She had polished her secretarial skills in

Spain while in college, as a backup for the possibility that she couldn't find a teaching job in the States. The money she had earned through Lakeworth Industries would be gobbled up fast by her mother's medical bills, so she could no longer afford to loll around the apartment and nurse her emotional wounds.

The alarm woke Felicia early the next morning, and she forced herself to get out of bed. If she allowed herself to ignore its ringing, she would waste another day in bed, and that she was determined not to do. She struggled with an almost overwhelming desire to give in to her depression and finally pushed back the covers, stuck her feet out and placed them on the floor.

Felicia went through her morning ritual of brushing her teeth, combing her hair and putting on her makeup, pondering the unfathomable question of just how much free will she had. If fate decided her behavior, there was no point in struggling to overcome her remorse. She might as well go back to bed and feel sorry for herself. But if she had free will, then it was up to her to overcome her misery, to get going this morning and make this day count for something.

Just as she was walking out of the bathroom, Felicia heard a rap at the door.

"Who is it?" she called, retrieving a dress from her closet to put on. She was a little puzzled about who would be dropping by so early.

"It's Roderick Bearstern," came the astonishing reply.

Felicia's heart did a somersault. Her knees became fluid. Her hands turned clammy. She pulled the neck of her dress up tight against her throat, as if the gesture would somehow protect her against an unwanted intruder.

As she slipped the garment over her head, Felicia felt fire burn her cheeks. The deep timbre of Roderick's voice called forth buried memories of a lingering, passionate kiss that had turned her world upside down, and she blushed shamefully at the recollection.

What was he doing here? He had sent her back to the United States, had paid her the salary she had coming, and she never expected to see him again. True, he had promised he wasn't going to give up trying to persuade her to be a model for him. But she had assumed that that was an empty threat prompted by ego. Roderick Bearstern was a man unaccustomed to being rejected.

"What do you want?" Felicia called through the door.

"Let me in and I'll tell you," Roderick said.

For a fleeting moment, Felicia harbored the impulse to bolt from the room, to run and hide. But she realized she was more afraid of her own weakness than she was of Roderick, and she was too humiliated to let him know it. If she refused to let him in, it would be tantamount to admitting the kiss in Spain had meant something to her. No. She would open the door, present a cool exterior and pretend she felt nothing more than disdain for him.

But Felicia was totally unprepared for the impact the sight of Roderick would have on her senses.

Unconsciously, she smoothed her hair in place and straightened her shoulders before opening the door. And there he stood! His dark eyes flashed with sprinkles of green, and Felicia's pulse pounded as his gaze raced over her. Her voice caught in her throat, and she couldn't speak as he brushed past her and closed the door behind him. She had almost forgotten how truly tall, powerful and imposing he was, how magnetic his presence, how overwhelming his personality. His dark hair looked almost coal black against the light blue shirt and white summer suit he wore. His olive complexion appeared ruddy. His square jaw had a determined set to it that unnerved her.

There was a lingering scent of a woody after shave lotion that almost made Felicia reel from giddiness. Why did he affect her this way?

"Hello, Felicia," Roderick said, his eyes devouring her from head to toe. "You're looking marvelous. May I sit down?"

"Help yourself," she said stiffly, not daring to loosen the tight leash she had harnessed on her emotions.

Roderick took a chair on one side of the room and motioned for Felicia to occupy the couch angled next to it.

"How was your trip back?" he asked.

"Fine. And yours?" she asked coolly.

"The same."

For a moment, they sat looking at each other, Felicia's feelings a knot of tangled uncertainties. She could hardly believe this was happening. She had spent all that time moping around, recovering from the emotional carnage she had experienced in Spain at this man's hands, and she was just pulling the pieces together at last. Then he had to show up, and no telling what kind of setback seeing him again would inflict on her.

"Why are you here?" Felicia asked bluntly.

"Because I need you, Felicia," Roderick said simply. "And you need me."

Felicia heard a rushing sound in her ears. A wide band tightened around her chest. Was it possible the kiss in Spain had actually meant something personal to Roderick? Was he here to tell her that he felt something for her?

"What do you mean?" she asked, her vision blurred from the sting of potential tears waiting to spill over if Roderick said the magic words she never thought she would hear.

"I thought it was obvious," Roderick said. "Do you mean you haven't been thinking about it? I sent you

115

back from Spain ahead of me to give you time to consider what we can offer each other, Felicia," Roderick said, his voice deep and charged with an emotion Felicia couldn't read.

"Which is?" she said shakily.

"Felicia, you're important to me."

"Really?" she choked, her heart almost bursting from happiness.

"Of course," he said persuasively. "I thought I had made that crystal clear to you. I've told you what a valuable asset you could be to me. You could launch a rebirth for Magic Glo cosmetics that would set the advertising world on its ear!"

The tears teetering on the edge of Felicia's lids turned to hot pools of anger and humiliation. She choked them back. She was both furious and mortified. She had thought for a fleeting second that Roderick was here to declare his love for her. She had hoped against hope that he had felt some of the same leaping bursts of joy she had experienced when he had held her in his arms in Spain. She had dared to imagine the two of them once again locked in each other's embrace in a fiery kiss of sheer ecstasy.

But all Roderick meant when he said he needed her was that she could be a big money-maker for his company.

"Don't you ever give up?" she asked caustically, turning her face away from him to hide the flash of shame that spread across her cheeks.

"I don't give up easily," Roderick said firmly. "You ought to know that by now."

"I wish you'd just go away and leave me alone," Felicia said in a strangled voice.

"I can't do that, Felicia," he said determinedly. "There's too much at stake for both of us. I can provide you with all the money you need for your mother's medical care. I can promise you a financial return on your time that you couldn't possibly earn anywhere else. You become the Magic Glo symbol, and you'll be worth a good deal of profits to my company in selling our cosmetics. In turn, you'll reap financial rewards beyond your greatest expectations. How can you say no?"

It wasn't easy to refuse knowing how much she could help her mother with the money she would earn. Most women would jump at the chance to have the kind of offer Roderick was laying at her feet. But she wasn't like most women. She had a very special reason for her reluctance, and he knew what it was. So she sat glumly on the couch, staring at her hands, saying nothing.

"Look at it this way, Felicia. You'll be doing a public service. We offer women hope. We show them the best-looking women in the world made up exquisitely to provide them a role model to emulate. Do you realize what benefits women derive from trying to keep themselves looking their best? They work to stay slim, keep in good health and remain youthful looking. They take pride in their appearance. It's healthy for all of us to be concerned about our looks. It makes us take steps that in the long run are beneficial to our overall well-being. What do you say?" Roderick concluded.

"Well . . ." Felicia dragged out the word, digesting Roderick's arguments, trying to find some flaw in them.

"You know it's true, Felicia, but you don't want to admit it because it would take some of the bite out of your hatred of modeling."

A bell went off in Felicia's brain that disturbed her. Could Roderick be approaching a roped-off area of her emotions on which she refused to trespass?

"I want to make you the symbol of glamour to women all over the world," Roderick went on. "I want to transport you from the world of an ordinary school-teacher to the magic world of make-believe that satisfies the dreams of women everywhere. I want to make

117

you the woman that other women look to for the spirit of glamour we all want in our lives. I want to see you on billboards, in magazine ads, on TV commercials. I want your picture to adorn every product in our line, so women who care about themselves and how they look can draw from you the confidence that, with our products, every women can look her best."

Roderick had been talking so fast and with such enthusiasm, Felicia found herself momentarily caught up in his description. She was on the point of believing there was something almost noble about being the Magic Glo Girl.

Then a wave of reality set in.

"No," she said lamely, her thoughts scattered and confused. When he spoke, it all sounded so right. But she couldn't let him sway her this way. Even though her arguments sounded hollow, she must keep in mind her basic feelings about modeling. "I've already given you my answer dozens of times. Can't you just accept that and leave me alone?" she pleaded.

"Never," Roderick said in a voice that threatened. "I've made up my mind to have you, and have you I will."

Felicia's resolve melted slightly in the face of the steely determination in Roderick's voice, and the knowledge of that weakened resolve frightened her. And then a little piece of Felicia died when she realized the limitation of what Roderick had just said. He was determined to have her, all right, but not in the way she would have eagerly welcomed. It was strictly business, nothing personal.

"I know how you feel," Roderick said. "But can't you see working for me would give you all the money you need for your mother's care? Don't you realize there's no place else you can get it? Look at the benefits I'm offering you. Besides a generous salary, as an added inducement I plan to set you up in a first-class apartment and dress you in fashionable designer clothes. If you're to become the symbol of glamour to women all over the world, you must have glamorous clothes and glamorous surroundings. You must live the part twenty-four hours a day."

"But I wouldn't be myself," Felicia choked.

"Nonsense," Roderick said. "Of course you would. You would be your *best* self. You'll still be Felicia Farr, but you'll be realizing your full potential for your destiny in life. Felicia, you were born to be a model. You're wasting your life as a schoolteacher, because you know deep in your heart you're living out somebody else's life script."

"But wouldn't I have to move to New York or California?" Felicia asked, testing for the first time her emotional reaction to the possibility of actually accepting Roderick's offer. "I want to live here, to be near my mother, in case she decides to see me."

"We can handle that," Roderick said confidently. "New Mexico can be your home base. We'll fly you to California to make our TV commercials. You may have to make some flights abroad for location photographs and promotions. We do want a cosmopolitan image for Magic Glo. It's sold all over the world. But I'll make it part of your contract that you can spend at least some of your time here." Roderick leaned forward in his chair and eyed Felicia intently.

"Any more objections?" he asked.

"Yes," she said. "I won't be exploited the way my mother was. She couldn't call her life or her time her own. She couldn't even admit to the public she had a daughter. Your father turned her into a slave for his company."

"I promise you nothing like that will happen to you," Roderick said reassuringly.

Felicia couldn't believe this was happening. Somehow Roderick Bearstern had walked in here less than half an hour ago and now had her on the verge of agreeing to do the one thing in life she had promised herself she would never do—model. She could no longer remember all the sound reasons she had for refusing him. His arguments were so convincing, so logical, she felt like a fool for refusing any longer.

When Roderick told her how much salary he guaranteed her the first year, Felicia made a quick mental calculation. "Well," she said at last, "I—I might be persuaded to model for you for one year . . . but no longer. I could probably earn enough for my mother's care in that time."

"I'll settle for that," Roderick said, ". . . for now."

A little bolt of apprehension darted through Felicia. There was a sinister ring to Roderick's words. He thought that once he had her under contract and she began making big money, she would get hooked on high living and keep working for him after the year was up. But he was forgetting one thing. She had never aspired to the glittering life of a top model. She was doing this only to earn money for her mother's medical care. And once that need was satisfied, she would have no reason to continue working for him beyond the expiration of her contract.

Felicia looked at Roderick with a pattern of desperation playing across her face. She was in a double bind. He wanted an answer, but she couldn't bring herself to say the words he expected to hear, the words that would plunge her into a world she hated but that would give her the means to help her mother. So, she merely nodded a mute agreement, choking back the tears waiting to spill over at the sound of her voice saying "Yes."

"You're not going to regret your decision." Rod smiled confidently. "Wait and see." He took her hands in his, and her flesh burned at his touch. Immediately, she regretted her decision. Working for Roderick would mean being around him regularly, loving him from a distance, hating him up close. What would that sort of conflict do to her? She had a friend in Spain who broke down from a similar experience. Too much stress, conflict and emotional upheaval had left her friend physically depleted, and she had ended up in the hospital, a nervous wreck. Would that happen to Felicia?

Roderick left soon after Felicia agreed to model for him, and she stood behind her apartment door, leaning weakly against it, wondering what the future held for her. How had she gotten from there to here, she wondered. At the end of school, she had been a simple schoolteacher, in charge of her own life, with a comfortable relationship with an easygoing, uncomplicated fellow. Now, she was on the verge of a glamorous career. Her life would not be hers to call her own, and she was hopelessly in love with a ruthless, unfathomable tycoon. It made no sense, this sudden change in her life. And it frightened her how drastically her future could change in such a short time.

Well, there was no looking back. She sighed. If she could just forget about her mother, forget her longing to see her, to talk to her, all this would be unnecessary. But she couldn't do it. No matter how rotten her mother had treated her, she couldn't turn her back on her own flesh and blood. She just wasn't made that way. Even if there was no chance her mother would ever see her, Felicia couldn't let the woman who gave birth to her languish in the depths of her despair without trying to help her. No, she was committed now, and she wouldn't back out of her agreement with Roderick, no matter how bitter she felt about it.

The next morning, Felicia received a call from a sophisticated secretary who requested her presence in a lawyer's office that afternoon. The lawyer had drawn up the contract, and Felicia signed it. She read it carefully, but she didn't understand all the complicated legal language. She would just have to trust to luck, she thought, that Roderick hadn't tricked her with some provision in the document he could use against her. As far as she could tell, the contract clearly specified her obligation to the company as one year, and that was the main provision Felicia had been worried about.

The ink was no sooner dry on her contract, than Felicia found herself in a dizzying spiral of glamour. Insisting that she live the image of an elegant Magic Glo symbol twenty-four hours a day, Roderick assigned a secretary to find a suitable luxury apartment for Felicia.

Felicia's head reeled when she surveyed her new living quarters.

Her apartment was a spacious, two-bedroom unit. The furnishings included a color TV with a giant projection screen and a sophisticated stereo system built into the living room wall. Powder blue carpeting ran throughout the interior, even in the bathroom, which included a private sauna. A balcony, lush with tropical plants and cactus from the desert overlooked an Olympic-size swimming pool located in the inner courtyard. The apartment complex, which rented only to affluent adults, also offered tennis courts, two smaller, heated swimming pools, an exercise room furnished with the finest in athletic equipment, and a racquet ball court. On the ground floor were an assortment of shops, a barber and hair stylist, a cocktail lounge and a small restaurant.

Felicia resolved that she must not succumb to the allure of this affluent life. She must remember this arrangement was temporary. The year would pass quickly, and she would find herself home again in her modest apartment, which she had insisted Roderick reserve for her. She had left her furniture and school clothes intact in her apartment, awaiting her return when the year was over. It was her reminder of reality, a way of keeping the current situation in perspective. While Roderick had wanted her to break all ties with her former ordinary existence, she had demanded this one concession. And he had given in.

Next, Felicia was taken to an exclusive shop owned by Magic Glo Cosmetics where she was measured by a top dressmaker. Yards of expensive fabric were carted out and draped around her to test her complexion and coloring for the best match of hues for her skin tones. She tried on a few basic designs to determine whether her figure looked best with an empire waistline, bare midriff, cut-back arm openings, full or straight skirt and long or short hem.

"She looks good in everything," the designer remarked with a note of admiration in her voice. "Her best colors are reds and blues, but even yellow looks good on her. We're not going to have any trouble at all making her a knock-out wardrobe."

Felicia had the rest of the day off to pick up a few personal belongings from her old apartment, and she was moved into her new surroundings by nightfall. She lay in the king-size bed, the blue velvet bedspread pulled back from the powder blue satin sheets. Layers of pink organza covered her body with one of the new negligees she had found in the closet. The secretary must have had an assistant who picked out all the lingerie Felicia found in the drawers of her bedroom. It was a little unnerving. She felt she was moving into someone else's apartment. Everything had been provided for her. The refrigerator was full of food, the bathroom was stocked with toilet articles, and the living room was decorated with paintings and plants.

At first Felicia hesitated using anything in the apartment she hadn't brought with her. But when she realized how little she had of her own things and how dependent she was on the supplies laid in by somebody else, she slowly got used to the idea that everything in the apartment had been put there for her use. So, she decided the only thing to do was to make herself at home.

The next morning, the secretary called for her again, and Felicia was driven to an exclusive beauty shop for a complete make-over. The secretary supervised every move of the makeup women, she gave the hair styler directions on how to cut and bleach her hair, and she stood over Felicia the entire time to make sure her instructions were carried out to the letter.

When Felicia left the beauty shop, her hair had been lightened to a soft platinum blond. It fluffed out around her face and gave her a soft, vulnerable, yet sexy appearance. Her eyebrows had been plucked thinner and arched farther from her nose. They, too, had been lightened to match her new hair color. The mascara on her eyelashes had been brushed thicker on the center lashes to give her a wide-eyed, innocent look. But a subtle eye shadow spread across her lids gave her a dewy-eyed come-hither expression that told of sensual ecstasy only dreamed of by most men.

"You do look like your mother," the secretary commented as she drove Felicia to an unspecified destination. Felicia held in her hand the photograph of her mother the secretary had used as her model for the new image Felicia had been given that morning. She felt a little sick inside at what she was doing. Roderick was trying to recapture the mixture of innocence and sexuality that her mother had projected. It was a combination that disarmed the women and made them want to copy her mother and appealed to the men and made them want to possess her mother.

It was an image; that's all it was. And that's all it had been with her mother . . . at first. But her mother must have begun to believe her own image, for she had been willing to sacrifice her own daughter to maintain it. Lucky for me, Felicia thought, that I know what a rotten life modeling really is. I'll never fall into the trap that snared my mother, she promised herself.

Felicia was so caught up in her own thoughts, she was only vaguely aware of where the secretary was taking her. They had parked the car outside some sort of studio, and the secretary was carrying a large box under her arm as she led her in the front door.

"Here, put this on," the secretary said, motioning to a dressing room door. "Feet first."

"Feet first?" Felicia said, her brow furrowed with a perplexed expression.

"So you don't mess up your hair," the secretary explained. "That's the way models always dress. Feet first."

"Of course," Felicia said vacantly. She reached out her hand, and the secretary draped a cool blue garment over her arm.

Felicia emerged a few minutes later in a form-fitting silk dress that plunged to the valley between her breasts and snuggled seductively around her hips and thighs. It had a wide sash that she had wrapped tightly around her small waist.

"I can't wear this," she protested, her cheeks burning with spots of red.

"Relax," the secretary said. "These are only test shots. It was the only dress I could find in the right color in your size on such short notice."

Felicia eyed her suspiciously. "Test shots?" she asked.

"You know," the secretary said. "To see which are your best angles, to see what kind of lighting to use, that sort of thing. It's kind of like a screen test."

Before Felicia could quiz her further, the door to the rear of the room opened, and Felicia felt a sudden lump form in her throat. Through the door strode Roderick Bearstern.

"Good afternoon," he said, and then he stopped dead in his tracks. "Beautiful, Mary. Just beautiful. I can hardly believe the resemblance." His eyes were studying her face intently.

Hearing the secretary's name, Mary, gave Felicia a little jolt. She was sure the woman had introduced herself on their first meeting, but she had paid no attention to the name. Her mind refused to believe all this was real. She wanted to stay as emotionally removed from what she was doing as possible. So she thought of the woman only as a secretary, never by anything so personal and concrete as her name.

Felicia had tried to hold all her feelings in check, to go through the motions without allowing herself to experience any personal sensations. But seeing Roderick was the one event from which she could not detach herself. And suddenly everything she was doing became painfully real. The woman to her side was no longer just a disembodied secretary. She was Mary, a flesh-and-blood woman who had been quite pleasant to Felicia. Felicia had to admit she liked Mary, in spite of herself.

And Roderick was here, near her, close to her, making her heart pound and her senses scream that she was crazy to love this man who wanted only one thing from her: her resemblance to her mother. He didn't even see her as a sexual conquest. He had proved that in Spain, when he had apologized for kissing her. All she was for him was a hunk of meat, just as her mother had been for his father, she thought miserably. When he looked at her, he saw dollar signs for his company. When she looked at him, she wanted to die because of the way she felt about him.

"Come on," Roderick said. "Let's see what we can do." He led her into a studio where a photographer dressed in dark pants and a shirt open to his navel slouched in one corner, loading a camera with a new roll of film.

"This is Bill," Roderick said, nodding to the photographer. "Bill, Felicia Farr."

Bill waved hello with one hand, his index finger slicing the air.

The next two hours ran into a blur of anxiety and bitterness for Felicia. While she wasn't posing for publication yet, she did have to pose with various Magic Glo cosmetics, and she found herself actually trying to look her best. What was it with her, anyway, she thought. If she pouted, frowned or screwed her face into unattractive grimaces, Roderick might conclude she just wasn't model material. He could very well pay her and never use her at all. But she had signed a contract with him, and she felt an obligation to do her best, regardless of how it pained her to model for him. After all, she did have her integrity. Roderick might think nothing of trying to trick her into getting what he wanted from her. But she would never have signed the contract if she had any intention of purposely messing up the photographs she knew she would have to pose for. She didn't believe in an eye for an eye and a tooth for a tooth.

What a pity that I don't, Felicia fumed silently to herself. It would be the perfect time to invoke that premise. If she looked dull, lifeless and shallow in the photographs, she might very well terminate her modeling career in a hurry. But regardless of how underhandedly Roderick had played with her, she couldn't trick him in return. Her conscience wouldn't let her. So, she smiled and thought pleasant thoughts to bring a sparkle to her eyes, and stood just as Roderick told her to.

Before long, Felicia was caught up in the sound of Roderick's voice. He was making verbal love to her, the way he had to Cheryl. At first she was so mesmerized by his intonations, she briefly forgot how much she despised him. All she could remember was the kiss in Spain and the melting of her heart when he had taken her in his arms. Every fiber of her being wanted to please him, to make him happy, to do exactly as he asked. A throbbing deep inside of her began to send hot flushes to her cheeks, and she felt her mouth begin to water. She could almost feel an overflow of sensual hormones surging through her as Roderick's voice caressed her, fondled her, carried her away on a cushion of promised fulfillment. It was the closest she had ever come to making love, and she wasn't even touching Roderick. There was a magic quality in his voice that transported her beyond the realm of the here and now, into a fantasy world where the two of them stood unclothed, looking across the space that separated them, their outstretched arms beckoning to each other, telling of their love and commitment.

The illusion was all in her mind, but it was prompted by the sound of Roderick's voice. As long as he whispered to her of sensuous pleasures, she was lost to the real world. She was totally oblivious to the clicking of the camera. All she heard and all she cared to hear were Roderick's protestations of love to her.

Then, all too soon, the shooting session was over, and the deep, intimate quality in Roderick's voice turned impersonal.

"That's all for today, Bill," he said, as he hustled Felicia out of the room.

"You were sensational," he whispered huskily as he and Felicia stood outside the door of the dressing room. As he looked deeply into her eyes, Roderick rekindled the magic for a moment. Felicia stood looking up at him, mouth parted, wet lips shimmering.

In that moment, Felicia was ready to forget everything and turn herself over to Roderick for whatever he desired. She stood immobile, too weak to move. No longer were she and Roderick separated from each other by a cameraman. He was in front of her now, only inches away, and the warmth of his body was all that kept her from shivering. His dark eyes held her hypnotized. Her arms ached to hold him. She longed to yell out, "Roderick, I love you!" She yearned for him to possess her . . . completely.

But just then, Mary appeared behind Roderick, and the magic spell was broken for good.

"How did it go?" Mary asked, her voice shattering the silence. Mary was reality, and Felicia felt totally ashamed of how she had lost touch with the real world in Roderick's presence.

Roderick turned, but not before a strange expression passed over his face. "Fine," he said in a strained voice that puzzled Felicia. Maybe he was just tired. Felicia was.

It wasn't until she was back in her new apartment, alone and completely away from Roderick, that Felicia realized the implication of what had happened today.

What a dope she was, she chided herself. She let herself lose her perspective completely. Roderick Bearstern had merely been doing his job. And he had been superb. No wonder Juan Carlos had been so eager to work with him. He was a genuis at getting the best out of his models. Felicia had seen him work with Cheryl, and today *she* had been the object of his concern.

Under his spell, Felicia had lost herself completely and had given him just what he wanted for his photographs. She had done so because, like all the rest of his models, she found him irresistible. For a while she had believed he really cared for her as a person, because he had told her so in the studio.

It was only now that she recalled his exact words, his tone of voice, the manner in which he had hypnotized her. And he had said the same things to her he had said to Cheryl in Spain. They were the words of a director, appealing to the emotional side of his model. The words had meant nothing to Roderick. They were merely rehearsed lines.

Felicia felt tears of shame spill over her lids and run down her cheeks. How could she have let herself believe, even for a minute, that Roderick might have meant even the tiniest portion of what he had said to her while she was posing? His words, "Magnificent, Love. Show me how much you want me, just as I want you. I want you to be mine forever. Say yes, and show me you mean it by your face . . ." echoed mockingly in her mind.

It was business, strictly business. How could Felicia endure a year of hearing Roderick talk to her like that, just so he could get the right expression from her for his photographs? It had been a mistake, a terrible mistake, to agree to work for him.

Just then, the telephone rang.

Was it Roderick? Why would he be calling this late?

Felicia almost decided not to answer it. But it was pointless to try to hide. He knew exactly where she was, and if he wanted to talk to her, he wouldn't let a little thing like her not answering the phone stand in his way.

"Hello," Felicia said feebly, picking up the blue receiver from its cradle on the bedside table.

"Hello," came a vaguely familiar masculine voice on the other end. "Miss Farr?"

"Yes . . ."

"This is Dr. Ambrewster."

"Dr. Ambrewster?" Felicia said, her throat threatening to close shut from excitement.

"Yes," he said. "I've been trying to reach you for the last few days. I couldn't understand why your number had been disconnected. Then, when it began ringing again, I got no answer."

"I moved recently," Felicia explained. "And

. . . and I've been out a lot the last couple of days. Is something wrong with my mother?" she asked, tension stealing through her body.

"No, nothing like that," Dr. Ambrewster reassured her. "It's the photographs you sent her. She's seen them and has agreed to see you."

"Really?" Felicia gasped, her voice a thin thread of disbelief. "She actually wants to see me?"

"I'm not sure *wants* is the exact word," Dr. Ambrewster corrected her. "She's nervous about the meeting, Felicia. But after looking at the photographs, especially when she saw how much you look like her, and then reading your letter asking to grant you just one visit, well . . . she told me she thought she was up to one visit. But she told me to tell you she can't promise anything more than that. And if she asks you to leave, you must agree to go."

"Oh, Dr. Ambrewster, thank you." Felicia sobbed, her voice cracking with emotion. "You don't know how long I've waited for this day. When can I come?"

"Tomorrow, if you can make it," he said. "She told me to call you Monday, but as I said, I couldn't get ahold of you. If you wait, she may change her mind again."

"I'll be there," Felicia said. "Will you tell her?"

"Yes, I'll tell her," Dr. Ambrewster said. "And, Felicia . . ."

"Yes?"

"Good luck. I hope it works out well for both of you."

"Thank you," Felicia cried, and with trembling fingers, placed the phone back on the cradle.

Chapter Seven

A nurse in a blue uniform walked briskly down the hall, her crepe soles whispering on polished vinyl. She carried a tray of pill cups each with its individual card to identify the correct patient. The hushed ambiance of the hospital was periodically broken by a discreet paging system calling a doctor's name.

Felicia stood outside Room 403. This was a moment she had dreamed of for many anguished years. Now that it had come, she wasn't sure if she knew how to handle it. Her palms were damp, her heart was racing, her stomach was tightened in painful spasms. Stage fright. Yes, she was having an acute case of it. What would she say to her mother? How should she act?

The woman in Room 403 was her mother, yet a stranger. How would that stranger greet her?

Felicia had a panicky impulse to turn and flee. Only

the knowledge of how bitterly she would later regret her cowardice kept her there.

Twice she reached for the door, twice drew back her icy fingers. Part of her was a lost, lonely little girl, desperately seeking the loving arms of her mother. Part of her was a bitter woman, despising her mother for deserting her. And yet another part of her was filled with compassion for the mother in 403 who had paid such a dreadful price for placing a career above her own daughter.

All of those different persons inside her were in deadly combat, turning her emotions into a shattered battlefield.

Somehow she pulled herself together, drew a shaky breath, said softly to herself, "This is what you've been wanting for so long, Felicia," and then pushed open the door.

The room was softly lighted, the drapes partly drawn. Felicia stood inside the doorway, clutching the box of flowers she had brought, as her eyes adjusted to the subdued lighting. She stared at the pale, thin woman resting on the partially elevated bed. The woman was partly turned away, gazing at the window.

A thousand hurting memories crowded through Felicia all at once, thrusting a lump into her throat, half blinding her with tears. Flashes of brilliant memories exploded in her mind. She saw a tall, beautifully poised woman, arms filled with gifts, bending to kiss her. Felicia felt again the childish shyness, her awkward self-consciousness, her inability, in the presence of this beautiful woman, to voice the torrent of words clamoring to be spoken. There were so many things she wanted to say . . . all the things she had thought about during the lonely nights. But, just as the shyness was beginning to melt, when she was about to find her tongue, the beautiful woman was hugging her again, saying a hurried goodbye, and promising to come again—promises that were broken more and more often as the visits became fewer and shorter, until there were none anymore. And Felicia was alone with her scrapbooks filled with pictures Felicia had cut out of magazines of the beautiful woman—the woman who had been her mother, but had become a stranger.

She remembered the awkward, self-conscious, ugly years of early adolescence, when she spent hours gazing at the pictures of her glamorous mother and comparing her own dumpy reflection in the mirror. Those had been the years when she had become convinced that the beautiful stranger was not really her mother, that she had been adopted. But then, as she grew out of the awkwardness into the slender grace of young woman-hood, she saw the unmistakable shadow of her mother's image in her face. And those were the years when the bitterness grew and deepened into a hard, clenched fist inside her as she tried to fathom how her mother could have forsaken her so cruelly. . . .

But those bitter thoughts were unable to completely crowd out the earlier memories, dim and faded now like a half forgotten picture scrapbook . . . memories of tender hands tucking her into bed, a sweet voice singing a lullaby, her mother dressing her, playing with her in the park. Those were the poignant memories that tugged at her heart, that brought tears, that kept her from hating Francine Farr completely. *Her mother must have loved her once,* she sometimes thought, almost desperately.

Now she wondered what kind of memories the pale woman on the bed was having. Was she, too, remembering the nursery many years ago, when she had held a small bundle of life close in her arms and loved her? Or was she remembering the hurried, awkward visits to a teenage daughter hidden away in a private Catholic school in Spain? And finally no more visits at all?

The woman on the bed had slowly moved her gaze from the window to Felicia. But her face gave no clue to her thoughts or feelings.

At last Felicia broke the strained silence. "I—I brought some flowers. Chrysanthemums. I hope you like chrysanthemums."

Her mother's gaze was fixed on Felicia's face. Slowly she nodded. "Yes," she murmured. "They're beautiful. Thank you."

Felicia swallowed with difficulty. "I'll—I'll put them over here." She moved to a dressing table.

"The nurse will put them in a vase," Francine said in a small, strained voice.

Felicia stood beside the dressing table for a moment, then moved around to the bed again. She thought, this is painful. We are total strangers.

The eyes of the two women, mother and daughter, gazed at each other across a vast chasm.

"How are you feeling?" Felicia asked politely of the stranger.

"Some better. I'm slowly regaining my strength. This morning, the nurse took me for a short stroll in the garden. They are good to me here. . . ." her voice faded.

The voice still had the beautifully modulated tones that Felicia remembered hearing on the TV commercials her mother had made for Magic Glo products. But it was thin now, and tired.

Felicia cleared her throat. "The doctor is pleased with your progress."

There was another awkward silence. We don't know what to say to each other, Felicia thought achingly.

Francine plucked at the bedcover. She touched her tongue to her lips. Tears moistened her eyes. "I . . . want to thank you," she whispered. She made a half-gesture at the room. "You are paying for all this. It costs so much. I don't know what I would have

. . . where I would have gone—'' Her voice halted. She bit her lip.

"It's all right." Felicia had a sudden impulse to pat the frail hand on the bed and asked herself, Why can't I?

"But it costs so much," Francine repeated. "Psychiatric care is so expensive."

"You mustn't worry about that. I can afford it."

Again a strained silence. Francine's eyes moved in the direction of a bedside table. Felicia followed her glance. She saw a framed photograph of herself, one of those Roderick Bearstern had made for her in Spain.

"It was a shock," Francine murmured, "to see that you had grown into such a beautiful young woman. I—I thought I was seeing some studio prints of myself." Her gaze moved to Felicia's face. "But it *is* you, Felicia."

It was the first time she had spoken Felicia's name. For a reason she couldn't analyze, hearing her mother speak her name brought a rush of hot tears, stinging her eyes, threatening to break the dam holding back the flood of emotions inside her.

At that point they were interrupted by a nurse bringing a hypodermic syringe on a tray. "I'm sorry," she said, "but it's nap time. The doctor doesn't want her to tire herself too much."

Felicia nodded, gather up her purse. The visit had been so unsatisfying, so bitterly reminiscent of the visits her mother had paid her in Spain—too short for them to say any of the important things. There was just time for polite, surface words and then goodbye.

But as she was leaving, Francine said, "Felicia—"

She turned. Their eyes met. The chasm was as wide as it had ever been; yet, Felicia had the sudden feeling that her mother was somehow reaching out across that wide gulf. "Could . . . could you come again?" Francine asked.

"Yes," Felicia replied quickly.

"Tomorrow, perhaps?"

"Yes, of course. Tomorrow."

Felicia left the building with a curious sensation of excitement. Her head was throbbing. Her stomach was churning to the point of nausea. The meeting had been a dreadful strain, an emotional holocaust. It had left her drained and shaken. And yet, somehow it had left her with hope, with an expectation of . . . what she didn't yet know. One thing was important: Her mother had not closed the door this time. She had invited her to come back tomorrow. Felicia had sensed in the invitation more than a feeling of obligation. There had been an undercurrent of a plea in her request that Felicia return.

She did return the next day, and the day after that, and again the day after that. Breaking down the barriers, crossing the wide gulf did not come easy or all at once. It was a dark and complex journey, with no road maps to follow.

"Restoring communication between an estranged mother and daughter is difficult," Dr. Martin, the psychiatrist who was consulting with Dr. Ambrewster, explained to Felicia in a meeting he had requested. "But I think it is important for you to continue to see your mother. The basic conflict that has brought on her depression is over her broken relationship with you. She will never get completely well until she resolves that conflict."

Nor will I, Felicia thought with a bitter stab. She hadn't broken down or succumbed to a depression, but there was a sickness inside her heart, too, a raw wound that could never heal until she could come to terms with her mother.

"How could she have done it, Dr. Martin?" Felicia asked, almost desperately. "You're a psychiatrist, trained in how people think. What could have possessed my mother to abandon me that way during my teenage years, when a girl needs her mother so much."

The psychiatrist looked at her thoughtfully. "It's not the first time a parent has placed his or her career above their children. In your mother's case there is more to it than that. But those are things *she* must tell you, if the healing process is to work."

The visits did indeed work a dramatic change in Francine's appearance. Felicia could see color returning to her mother's face. The traces of regal beauty still remained in her ravaged features and began to blossom again like a flower that has been watered. She grew stronger and was able to walk in the garden on the hospital grounds with Felicia. During those walks, when they were alone together, away from the sterile atmosphere of the hospital room, they talked of many things. Gradually the outer layers of restraint and defenses melted away until they were finally able to discuss feelings close to their hearts.

"I know this will be hard for you to accept, Felicia, but I never stopped loving you, in spite of what happened—"

"I—I find that hard to believe," Felicia said frankly. "How could a mother who really loves her daughter send her away to a foreign country and pretend to the world she doesn't exist?"

They sat on a bench in the garden. Francine was gazing at her with tear-filled eyes, struggling with words that were as painful to her as knife thrusts. "I made a mess of my life, Felicia," she confessed miserably. "I guess I'm not the first person who has done that. Unfortunately, when a person screws up his or her life, they often hurt people close to them. In this case it was you. Why did I do it? Because I'm a weak person," she admitted bitterly. "I never had the strength or character or guts or whatever it takes to live my own life. I lived my life in other people. I let them tell me what to do. I had no identity of my own.

"There's a lot about me, about my background, that you don't know," her mother continued. "I want to tell you, though it isn't easy. I'm not telling you this because I expect you to forgive me. I . . . I just hope that perhaps it will help you to understand me and why I did what I did. . . ."

Felicia's emotional responses ranged from bitterness to compassion, from sadness to shock as she listened to her mother's halting words.

"Of course, you don't know anything about my childhood or your grandparents," Francine told her. "We were dirt poor. My father was a coal miner in Kentucky. He was a despicable man, a drunkard and a wife-beater." Now Francine's words were etched in a bitterness of her own. "I never had a daddy who loved me. I knew only fear and hate toward him. He mistreated my mother and my brother and sister and me in horrible ways. My mother died before she was thirty-five, worn out from work and abuse. My sister died from typhoid before she was fifteen. My brother ran away from home. He was the smart one, I guess. We never heard from him anymore. I got married the first time when I was fifteen. I didn't know anything about love or being married. If a girl doesn't have a daddy who's kind and loving, she grows up hungry for a man's love but never sure anyone can love her. She's never sure who she is. At least that was how it was with me."

Francine paused for a moment, gathering her strength to go on with the painful story. Then she said, "I was fifteen when some friends in our little coal-mining town heard about a beauty contest at the county seat. You were supposed to be sixteen to enter, but I was tall for my age and could easily pass for sixteen. I didn't know I was pretty. Nobody had told me. But my friends talked me into entering the contest, and I won first place. They had a big celebration. The beauty contest was part of it. And there was a street dance. There was a string band. A fellow in the band played guitar and sang. Jeff Parker was his name." For a moment a sad smile touched Francine's lips. "Jeff asked me to marry him. I said yes—anything to get away from my home. Jeff was your real father, Felicia."

Felicia suddenly felt close to tears. It was like seeing doors open to her past. And as the doors opened, one by one, her mother was becoming a real person instead of the distant, beautiful stranger—a real person whose life had been a tragedy.

"You never knew your real father," Francine told her. "I think Jeff would have been a good daddy for you. He had a kind, sweet nature. But I wasn't his wife long enough to really get to know him. We weren't married a year before you were born. And you weren't a week old when Jeff was killed in a car wreck coming home one night from playing at a dance.

"There I was," Francine said, "a sixteen-year-old widow with a baby to support. I didn't have anyone to turn to. I got a job doing the only thing I could handle—waiting tables in a roadside café." She smiled wryly. "It was one of those places people talk about, where the waitresses got handled more than the menus. But I had this hunger to be loved. I'd go out with truck drivers, salesmen, Saturday-night cowboys—anyone who'd ask me. I guess I was looking for something I never had: a daddy's love. I worked at that place for nearly a year when I met your stepfather, Edmund Farr.

"Edmund was different from the men I'd been exposed to. He wasn't country like we were. He'd worked for some big advertising companies in New York. He was traveling through on his way to California, temporarily between jobs. I guess he was smart enough to see the potential in me as a model. He hung

140

around town for a week, taking me out, and he convinced me to marry him and go on to the West Coast with him.

"Edmund was a lot older than the guys I'd known. He was polished, sophisticated, and I was just a naive country girl. I don't think I ever really loved him." She shrugged. "I didn't know what love was. But I desperately wanted to please him. It was so important for people to like me, for somebody to care for me. That was the only way I had any identity.

"Looking back, I'm sure Edmund never loved me. He wanted me for a bed partner, and he didn't want to be guilty of violating the Mann act by taking an unmarried young woman across state borders for immoral purposes. But more important than that, he saw the possibility of selling me as a model for his own profit.

"He made a slave out of me," Francine said bitterly. "This isn't pretty, Felicia, but I have to tell you all of it. At first, the only modeling jobs he could get for me were sleazy figure model assignments for photographers who sold their material to men's sex magazines. At the same time, he had me going to a modeling school where I learned how to use makeup, to develop poise, to get rid of my country accent. Gradually the modeling assignments became more respectable, and the pay got better. Edmund knew his way around the advertising field. He was a born promoter. He knew that the average models didn't make that much money. He was shooting for the top with me—magazine covers, TV commercials. He had some pretty good contacts. Finally we hit it big with the Magic Glo campaign. I became 'Francine—the Magic Glo Girl.'"

She smiled sadly. "Can you picture *me*, Felicia, a country girl who'd worn feed sacks made into dresses when I was growing up, suddenly having all that fame, making all that money. I was terrified the whole time. I was utterly dependent on Edmund. He told me how to pose, how to conduct myself in public . . . how to think.

"How did all this affect your life, Felicia? Well, to begin with, Edmund resented you from the beginning. He disliked having a child in tow, and he was impatient about the time I spent with you. He wanted me to be working on my modeling career twenty-four hours a day. He knew the earning power of a model is short— only a few years, while she's young. As my career picked up, demanding more and more of my time, he began insisting we put you in a boarding school. He pointed out how hard my life was on you, how much I was gone from home and had to leave you with nursemaids. He said I was being selfish, that a good mother would put her child's welfare above her own. He could be very convincing. And, as I said, I had no mind of my own. He could talk me into doing anything. He told me that a young girl would have all kinds of advantages by going to a first-class European girls' boarding school. She would have a polish and sophistication she wouldn't get here at home. The truth was," she said sadly, "he wanted me to keep a youthful image. He didn't want 'Francine—the Magic Glo Girl' to be seen in public with a teenage daughter giving her age away. But I didn't admit that to myself at the time. I just let him talk me into what he wanted, and I told myself it was for your own good in the long run."

"Couldn't you have visited me more often!" Felicia exclaimed, suddenly giving vent to the bitterness that had smoldered in her so long. "Didn't you know how much I needed my mother?" Her voice broke and tears blinded her.

"It became so painful for me," Francine said, crying now, too. "Every time I saw you, I wanted more desperately to take you home with me. You have no conception of how hard it was for me to walk off and leave you there. They kept crowding my schedule more and more, flying me all over the world, making TV spots, posing for photographers. I'm sure that's when my emotional stability began to crumble. I was living on coffee and amphetamines to keep going, and tranquilizers to sleep. And all the while, I was struggling with my guilt and conflict over you.

"It was during those years that I lost what feeling I had for your stepfather—what might have once passed for love. I became like an empty puppet, allowing him to pull the strings."

Felicia wiped her tears and frowned. "I've always blamed John Bearstern, the president of the Magic Glo corporation for taking over your life. Wasn't he as much to blame as my stepfather? He controlled your life to make a profit for his business."

Francine shook her head. "No, John was not at fault, and you mustn't blame him. The fault lay squarely with my weakness and your stepfather's cold nature and ruthless ambition. John Bearstern was a fine man . . . a man I respected and . . . and loved."

"Loved?" Felicia echoed, astonished.

"Yes. But not in the way you might think. I'm sure he never knew of my feelings. He was married, you see. He had his own cross to bear—a wife who was an alcoholic, in and out of hospitals and sanitariums. But he was loyal and faithful to her. I did love him, though. He was the only man I ever felt about that way." She sighed. "But that did not concern you. What *did* concern you was that I stopped visiting you altogether. I no longer had the strength. Seeing you only made my conflict more painful. I began hiding from you and from the hurt. It was the start of more and more hiding until I gradually hid from the world. After your stepfather died and my age, plus my breakdown in health, ended my modeling career, I became more and more of a recluse."

"You refused to see me when I came back to the States," Felicia said accusingly. "I tried so hard to penetrate the wall you had built around yourself. It was so important for me to see you. Why, after all these years, did you still refuse to see me, your own daughter?"

"Isn't it obvious?" Francine choked. "I was so ashamed. I felt terribly guilty. I didn't want to face you, to have to admit that I had deserted my own daughter. So I hid behind my own misery. I kept thinking the pain would eventually go away, and I'd learn to live with myself again. But then I found out you were paying for my hospitalization, and I felt more wretched than ever. It wasn't until your picture came that I finally was forced to face myself. You were no longer just a blur in my memory, a young girl with a tear-stained face. You had become a woman, a very beautiful one. You reminded me of myself when I was younger. I knew I'd never get your face out of my mind. So, I decided to see you. Because of the psychotherapy I've had here, I somehow found the courage to face up to what I'd done. I—I wanted to ask you something. . . ." Francine's voice trailed off.

"What's that?"

"I—I know I don't deserve it, but can you ever find it in your heart to forgive me, Felicia?" Francine sobbed.

"Mother," Felicia said hoarsely, her vocal cords thick from emotion. "I didn't come here for you to beg my forgiveness. I wanted to see you for my own interests. How do I explain it? My father died when I was so young. I saw so little of you after you sent me away. I needed to know what kind of person my mother was, what she looked like now, the sound of her voice. . . . It's a matter of understanding my identity. And you're part of that identity. Does that make any sense?"

Francine nodded. "Indeed it does. It especially

makes sense to someone like me—a woman who has never had an identity of her own."

Felicia could no longer hold back a flood of her own tears. She found herself in her mother's arms, held close and warm, for the first time since she was a little girl. She cried for the pathetic, tormented life her mother had lived. She cried for the little frightened country girl terrified of her own father. She wept for the country boy musician, her own father, that she had never known. And mostly she shed tears for her own lonely years without her mother.

The tears had a purging effect, washing away the bitterness and at last closing the terrible chasm that had separated her from her mother for so many years.

Once the barriers between them were swept away, Felicia and her mother were able to talk easily, to tell each other of their deepest feelings and to catch up on the years they had been apart. Francine was eager to hear about those missing years when she had been estranged from her daughter. She begged Felicia to tell her about her schooling, her teenage years and how she had eventually moved back to the United States.

Felicia described the conventlike atmosphere at the Catholic school in Spain, how carefully she had been chaperoned, how naive she had been about boys, never having dates like her peers in this country. She talked about her ambition to become a schoolteacher, how she had gone to college in Spain, returned to the States, was issued a temporary teaching certificate by the state of New Mexico and found her first position in a high school here. She attended night school to meet the requirements for a permanent teaching certificate in New Mexico.

Inevitably her story had to bring her to the present, to Roderick Bearstern and her acceptance of a modeling career with the Magic Glo corporation.

That part she found difficult to put into words. She

145

felt embarrassed to talk about Roderick Bearstern. Her feelings were too confused and turbulent on *that* subject.

And she was reluctant to tell her mother about Roderick's plan to make her the new Magic Glo Girl. That had been her mother's position. Having to reveal that she was stepping into her mother's shoes made her uncomfortable. It seemed cruel, as if she were flaunting her youthful good looks and health before the fallen queen. And yet she couldn't keep her modeling work hidden from her mother. Obviously she couldn't earn enough money teaching school to pay for this expensive psychiatric care. And the time was going to come when her mother would pick up a magazine and see Felicia in a Magic Glo Cosmetics ad.

So, she had to make a clean breast of the matter.

She fully expected her mother to be upset by Felicia's accepting a modeling job, and with the Magic Glo corporation at that, after what it had done to Francine's life. But her mother's reaction was surprisingly affirmative.

"A modeling career can be what you make of it, Felicia. It wasn't modeling or the Magic Glo people who wrecked my life. It was my own lack of character. And if Roderick Bearstern is anything like his father, I'm sure he's a fine man."

"I—I'm not sure what he is," Felicia stammered, her face turning pink. "He's a very forceful man, used to having his own way about things. . . ."

"But quite attractive?"

"Y-yes," Felicia admitted, growing more flustered.

"Sounds very much like his father." Francine was giving her daughter a thoughtful look. "Are you in love with him, Felicia?"

The unexpected question shattered what was left of Felicia's composure. "Oh, mother! I—I don't know.

He does have more than his share of charm and masculine appeal. No, I don't love him. I hate him!"

"Do you really? Hate him, I mean?"

For the first time, Felicia saw a glint of amusement in her mother's eyes. It was almost worth the acute state of embarrassment Felicia was suffering.

Then with a sad smile, Francine murmured, "I would be so happy, Felicia, if you succeeded where I failed—if you handled this modeling career on your own terms, standing up for your own rights. And if you are in love with Roderick Bearstern . . . that it have a happier ending for you than the secret love I've carried in my heart for his father all these years."

Felicia squeezed her mother's hand. "Thank you, Mother. But I don't want a modeling career. It's too demanding. I only want a simple life as a schoolteacher. I agreed to a year's contract with Magic Glo in order to see that you had good medical care. As for any romance between Roderick Bearstern and myself . . . well, first of all, he's not in love with me. He's only in love with his corporation. He sees me as an index to his profits. And my feelings . . . well, I'll admit I'm attracted to him in a physical way. But that doesn't add up to a lifetime commitment. I'm sure it isn't the kind of feeling you have for his father."

She wondered why her words had a hollow ring.

The next day, Felicia was scheduled to see a TV film she had shot in New York. Roderick had arranged to meet her in his office, where he would play it back on his video-cassette player. Felicia was so wrapped up in her pleasure over her budding relationship with her mother, that she didn't even mind the prospect of having to confront Roderick again. But she was little prepared for a new crisis in their relationship.

"Good morning," she said cheerily, as he opened his

office door for her. "You're looking fit," she observed, her eyes appreciatively taking in the dark suit which he filled out so magnificently.

"And so are you," Roderick said huskily. "Both on film and in person. Come on in."

"Thank you," she quipped and walked across the plush carpet to an overstuffed chair angled toward the TV screen, which sat in one corner of the room. As she passed Roderick, she caught the musky scent of his woody after shave lotion. She felt almost dangerously wicked. It was a strange mood she was in, brought on by the events of the last few days in getting to know her mother, and this morning she was prepared to take on the world and come out on top. And that included any confrontation with Roderick Bearstern. She felt an impulsive urge, which she resisted, to throw her arms around his neck, give him a big kiss and then sit nonchalantly in the chair, as if nothing had happened. That would really set him on his ear, she chuckled to herself.

It was a heady feeling, to have the upper emotional hand. Right now, she was reeling from a sense of power. Roderick could do nothing to upset her today, because she had grown strong and self-assured this last week. She knew who she was, what she wanted and how to get it.

Or so she thought.

"The commericial is superb, Felicia," Roderick said, his eyes trailing up Felicia's crossed legs.

"It should be." Felicia smiled wryly. "It only required twenty-five takes!"

Roderick brushed her comment aside. "Some professionals require more for a perfect piece of film. You have a real natural talent. Let me show you what I mean."

Roderick pushed a button on a little black box in his hand, and the TV screen lit up. For a moment, Felicia thought she was looking at her mother. Then she realized she was seeing herself as millions of TV viewers would see her on her first commercial. She was fascinated by her own image extolling the virtues of Magic Glo cosmetics. But it was more a fascination of horror than one of admiration. She was actually on the verge of being launched into a new career that could very well engulf her and suck her into its mire before she realized what was happening to her.

Already she had seen the first hint of what her new life could do to her. She had been forced to give up her simple apartment for a luxury suite that overwhelmed her. Her makeup and hairstyle had been chosen for her. She had to spend hours making sure she was always perfectly groomed. She had been forced to give up her teaching career. It was frightening, starting this new venture, not knowing where these first steps would take her, or what the future held. She was losing control of her life, and she didn't like that.

"Well, what do you think?" Roderick asked when the screen went black. "Weren't you sensational?"

"I—I don't know," Felicia stammered. "It's hard to be objective about myself. It's like looking at someone else, yet not being able to divorce myself completely from that other person."

"Well, you can rely on my judgment." Roderick's dark eyes settled on Felicia's face. Disturbed, she looked away.

Roderick continued. "You'll be interested to know that based on the results of these preliminary TV commercials and some market surveys we've just completed, we're going to launch a new Magic Glo line in the fall, which will be centered around the new Magic Glo Girl."

Felicia's brows drew together in a frown of displeasure. "I'm not sure if I like the sound of that. Won't it be taking up a lot more of my time?"

"Your time belongs to me for the next year," Roderick reminded her in a steely voice. "Remember, when you signed that contract, I bought you for the next year."

Her face flamed. "You make me sound like a prostitute!"

"Hardly," he retorted coldly. "I'm offering you more success, money and fame than you ever dreamed of."

"In exchange for what? My life?"

He shrugged. "If you want to put it that way. People who succeed do it because they are dedicated. They make sacrifices. They give of themselves."

"That's fine," she retorted, "if they're pursuing their own goals. My goal is to be a good teacher. Circumstances have let you trap me in this situation . . . but it's only temporary."

Bearstern gave her a look of angry frustration. "You can be exasperating and stubborn. You're like a child who needs a good spanking."

Her eyes blazed. "You'd better not!" she warned.

"Only a figure of speech," he growled. But the expression in his eyes told her he would relish making his threat a reality.

He paced restlessly around the office, making the air crackle with the electric charge of his energy. "You baffle me, you know that?" he stormed. "Can't you see the opportunities that could open up to you? I can practically guarantee you a part in a TV network show or a Hollywood contract if you'll work with me on this new Magic Glo promotion and sign a new contract when your first year is up."

"And if I refuse to pose for your new line of cosmetics?" Felicia challenged defiantly, her chin raised.

"Let me remind you," Roderick said, his voice edged with steel, "that you're working for *me*. If I order you to pose for this new line, you'll pose for it. If I decide on a big, international buildup of the new Magic Glo Girl, you'll cooperate. You seem to forget that because I hold the purse strings, I also hold the strings on you."

"Just like a puppet, huh?" Felicia said bitterly. "And what if I refuse?"

"Not only will I cut off the funds," Roderick growled, "I'll take you to court. You signed a legal, binding contract. Where are you going to get the money to hire a lawyer to fight me?"

"You're despicable, do you know that?" Felicia said angrily, hot tears of wrath burning her eyes.

"I am merely exercising my rights under a contract which you freely signed," Roderick said with a wicked grin. "So how does that make me a villain?"

Felicia was so infuriated that any answer she might have hurled at him stuck in her throat.

"And just when do I have to report for my next assignment?" Felicia asked acidly.

"Thursday," Roderick said, a look of triumph spreading across his face. "We'll fly you to New York for some preliminary shots for our new package design." He paused. "Just keep reminding yourself how much all this money has done for your mother."

Felicia shot Roderick a murderous glance, yanked up her purse off the floor and marched out of the office in a huff. She rode in silence in the taxi back to her apartment.

Once inside, Felicia was swept with a wave of guilt and anger mingling in a rush of emotional torment that set her eyes stinging with tears and her lips trembling with near hysteria. She threw her purse across the room and barely missed knocking over a tropical plant sitting near the balcony door.

What was it that disturbed her so about what she was doing? she wondered. She sat down on one of the velvet chairs and slipped her feet out of her shoes. She ran her feet across the thick blue carpet, luxuriating in the feel of the soft pile.

Felicia looked around, Roderick's words echoing in her ears. She was surrounded by opulence. Most women would jump at the chance for the life she had had thrust upon her. Why was she so adamant in her refusal to enjoy herself?

Guilt. That was it. Somehow, it always came back to guilt. But what did she feel guilty about? She had seen Francine, had found her very likable, was beginning to establish her own identity. And heaven knows she had been the best daughter she could be under the circumstances. So why was she resisting Roderick so much?

Fear. Maybe it was that, more than guilt. She was afraid of turning out like her mother: a lonely, frightened woman hiding behind a rock wall of shame.

Felicia's troubled thoughts tumbled in and out of her consciousness with lightning speed. She couldn't grab ahold of any of her subconscious motivations long enough to examine them clearly. She was being irrational, and she didn't understand why.

Wearily, Felicia rose from the chair. She wandered around her apartment aimlessly for a while, looking in the refrigerator but deciding she was too upset and confused to eat. She straightened a few items on her dresser, and her hand fell on a package she had almost forgotten about. Her mother's birthday was approaching. Felicia had bought a double picture frame for a present, planning to include photographs of herself and her mother that she had obtained from the Magic Glo files.

Better put the pictures in now, she thought, and wrap the present. It would be ready for her to take to the hospital when she returned from the trip to New York.

She gazed at the photograph of her mother, at the gentle curve of her mother's generous mouth, the platinum-blond hair, the large eyes with their long lashes. She slipped Francine's picture into the left side of the double frame. Then she picked up a photo of herself, one that Roderick had taken of her while they were in Spain. Again she was shocked at the resemblance she bore to her mother. The moment she placed her photograph beside her mother's she felt a wave of anxiety. Her throat tightened, her breathing became labored. Her hands shook.

"What is it?" she demanded of herself out loud. "What's bothering me?"

Then suddenly, like a blinding flash illuminating the darkness in her mind, she realized why she had resisted for so long what Roderick had said was her destiny.

Why hadn't she realized it before? The sudden insight infused her with a giddy feeling. It also imbued her with a newfound courage to formulate and carry out a plan that would surely infuriate Roderick Bearstern while establishing once and for all her own identity as Felicia Farr, and not a carbon copy of Francine Farr.

Chapter Eight

It was one of those hot New York days when stifling heat radiated up from the streets and tall buildings, suffocating the city.

Felicia was grateful to be engulfed by cool air when she entered the air-conditioned building where she was to meet Roderick and the photographer.

Roderick, she thought with a chuckle of private glee, was in for the surprise of his life.

She felt quite smug this morning. She flicked her head to one side, and her short, dark blond curls bounced freely. It was quite a change from the long platinum tresses she had worn the last time Roderick had seen her. She couldn't wait to see the expression on his face when he saw her transformed back into Felicia Farr. She was no longer the reincarnation of her mother. She had even changed her makeup. Gone were the widely arched eyebrows that had given her that wide-eyed look. She had penciled in her natural browline, which was less dramati: and a bit closer to her eyes. She had dyed her hair back to its natural color and had cut it shorter. She had also dressed in an outfit more befitting her own personality. While the dress was stylish, it had simpler, more fluid lines than the formfitting wardrobe Roderick had ordered for her.

At last, thought Felicia, she felt free, free to be herself. All those years she had longed to see her mother, she had struggled to establish her own identity. There had been a cloudy haze over who and what she was. But now that she had seen Francine, had met her face to face, had come to know what kind of person she was, Felicia finally had the freedom to be her own person. That was what had been bothering her so much about modeling. Roderick had not wanted to photograph her as herself. He had wanted to turn her into her mother. And her subconscious rebelled at the thought of being something she wasn't, especially her mother.

Felicia had to be herself, no matter what the cost. She had been willing to submit to Roderick's demands about her hair and makeup before she had seen her mother because her own identity was still weak and unformed. And she needed the money so badly for her mother's care. But in the last few days, Felicia had come to know herself and to understand what she wanted out of life. And one thing she did not want was to be the new image of her mother.

Felicia entered the photo studio, and the secretary directed her to Roderick's office. It seemed he had a private office in every city in America, she observed. And why not? His company could certainly afford it.

Another secretary told her to join Roderick in the studio where the photographs would be shot.

Felicia's heart began pumping faster. She had no idea

how Roderick would react when he saw her. But she knew he would have something to say about the change in her. And she anticipated it would be negative.

Felicia's breathing became rapid and shallow as she rounded the doorway and saw a dark head of hair bent over in conference with a smaller, pale man who must be the photographer.

A large backdrop of colorful swirls of reds and pinks stood ready for the Magic Glo Girl, and a table nearby held the new line of products. Electronic strobe lights were in position.

Felicia cleared her throat. The two heads parted, and dark eyes set in an olive complexion swung in her direction.

Roderick gave her a cursory glance, dismissed her with a disdainful look and resumed his conversation. Then suddenly, he stopped in midsentence, jerked his head toward her in a fast double take, and his brown eyes blazed black with fury.

"Felicia!" he bellowed. "What have you done to yourself!"

Felicia set her jaw at a determined angle. She was surprised at her own courage in facing up to Roderick.

"I've turned me back into myself," she said evenly, her eyes narrowing, a visual cue to the steely resolve within her.

"Your hair, your makeup!" Roderick grumbled. "It's all wrong."

"No," Felicia said. "It's right. Right for me. I'm through being Francine Farr the Second. From now on, I'm going to be me, whether you like it or not!"

"Is that a wig?" Roderick demanded, devouring the space between them with long strides. He reached up to pull off the short, curly locks.

"Ow!" Felicia squealed. "No, it's not a wig. It's my own hair. Now stop that!"

156

The photographer on the other side of the room put his camera down and sat watching the proceedings with an amused look on his face which said he had witnessed many squabbles between models and company executives.

"Why, Felicia?" Roderick asked angrily.

"I told you," Felicia said, a note of exasperation tinging her voice. "I'm not going to give up my identity in order to let you make me into another Francine Farr. If you're going to use me as the Magic Glo Girl, you're going to have to photograph me as myself."

Roderick shook his head. "But the plan is to bring Francine Farr back."

"I refuse to be the ghost of my mother," Felicia said, stubbornly holding her ground.

Roderick's frown was like a dark thundercloud. He stared at Felicia with a penetrating, ruthless look. Then he mumbled something Felicia didn't understand, and he held another conference with the photographer.

A few minutes later, much to her surprise, Felicia found herself before the camera. Automatically, she held the various Magic Glo products as Roderick directed.

After the shooting session was completed, Felicia realized for the first time what her impulsive action might cost her. She was still dependent on Roderick's money for her mother's hospital care. If he decided to fire her for her refusal to cooperate with his plans, his legal department could no doubt find some grounds to terminate her contract.

The way Roderick stalked out of the studio without another word to her convinced her that he might be considering such action.

She must have been out of her mind to take such a chance, she thought with a shudder. Why had she been so reckless? What had driven her to be so brazen? It was as if some perverse impulse was driving her to deliberately antagonize Roderick Bearstern.

The next day, Felicia received a phone call from Roderick's secretary instructing her to be in his office within an hour. She dressed with trembling fingers. She felt a cold knot in the pit of her stomach as she took a cab to his office building.

Felicia arrived at the office much meeker than she had been the day before. When the secretary led her into Roderick's office, she sat quietly in a chair, rehearsing an apology. Perhaps if she emphasized how much she needed this money for her mother's medical care, he might give her another chance.

The door opened, and Roderick's huge frame entered through a side door. He was carrying the familiar manila envelope which Felicia knew contained prints of the previous day's shooting.

She studied his expression for a clue to his mood. What she saw did not reassure her. His brown eyes were cold, his square jawline hard. He sat behind his desk and scowled at her. Then he tossed the envelope on the desk. "Look at them."

Her mouth was dry. "What?"

"The photographs. Look at them."

Felicia took them limply, all her reserves of energy drained from her. She fumbled through the prints. "They . . . they don't look too bad," she said weakly.

He rose and moved to the window. He stared at the traffic ten stories below. "No," he muttered, "they're not bad. Not bad at all." He shook his head slowly. "I wouldn't have believed it."

"I . . . I don't understand," she faltered.

He turned, giving her another black look. "What I mean is that you do have a personality of your own. A

158

look of your own. And it's good. Far better than I'd first thought when you sprung this transformation on me. You realize what this means, don't you?"

She shook her head numbly.

"Well," he said, "it means I have to revamp my entire plans for this new promotion. All along I've thought of it in terms of a Francine Farr revival. I'd planned to make you look as much like your mother as possible. Perhaps that was wrong. I didn't want to admit it, but you could have a point." He jabbed a finger at the photographs. "The proof is right there. I had no idea you'd look so good."

"Then—"

He held up his hand. "Wait. Don't get any big ideas, yet. I want more proof. We'll have to televise you with this new image. I have to have some conferences with my advertising people."

He began pacing the floor, talking rapidly. "You have the scrubbed, wholesome look of the girl next door, but you are still ravishing and sexy. The look of the Eighties. Natural beauty achieved through the subtle use of Magic Glo cosmetics. We can build an entire campaign around that theme and advertise you all over the world. You'll demonstrate to women how they can achieve the look of the Eighties. And we'll do it through an entirely new Magic Glo symbol—Felicia Farr. Not an imitation of her mother, but a new symbol for a new decade."

He swung around and gave her one of his dynamic looks that shot a tingling sensation through her body. "I'm big enough to admit when I've been wrong. And I might have been wrong all along. All of my life, I've been so dazzled by the memory of your mother's beauty. She was my dream woman when I was first starting in this business, when my father was still head of the corporation before he retired. I couldn't get her out of my mind. Whenever I thought of Magic Glo, I automatically thought of Francine Farr. It was a fixation with me, an obsession. When I looked at you, I saw a reproduction of Francine. Perhaps it took a bit of a jolt to make me see you as a completely different individual. And that doesn't take anything from your potential. Everything about you that I said before still goes. You have all the potential to become the new Magic Glo Girl, in your own right. And you can go on from there to the other successes I mentioned—a TV series, a Hollywood contract. All of it can be yours, Felicia."

Felicia sat hypnotized by Roderick's words. He was caught up in a spiral of enthusiasm so compelling that she was transfixed. Slowly, the meaning of her victory became a reality to her. She felt a flush of triumph, but something vastly more important than that. Now she truly felt she had established her identity as an individual. At last she knew who she was. "I—I have no ambition to be a star, as I told you," she said quietly. "I just want to fulfill my contract and go back to the life I had before."

"I have you under lock and key for this next year, at least," Roderick said. "And whether you like it or not, I'm going to make the most of you!"

Felicia was aware that she was still in bondage as much as before. How could she let herself fall in love with a man this ruthless, a man who saw her only as a promotional object, whom he would use and exploit in every way he could to earn more profits for his company? The heartbreaking truth—and she must live with it—was that she had fallen in love with him. It would be torture to see him again and again this next year, to pose as he directed, to be at his beck and call. The only way she could bear the coming year would be to remind herself constantly that she was doing this for her mother. Finally, the year would be over and she would never see him again.

Later that week, she was back in her swank apartment in New Mexico. In the evening she put on one of her designer lounging pajamas. She was surrounded with luxury. But she frowned with dismay. Too bad she couldn't enjoy all this while it lasted, she thought dismally.

A knock at the door brought her to her feet. A visitor might be just the thing to take her mind off herself. She opened the door to a sandy-haired man with blue eyes.

"Don!" Felicia exclaimed.

"Hi," he said with a broken smile. "Can I come in?"

"Sure," Felicia said warmly, glad to see someone from the ordinary world for a change.

Don stepped across the threshold. His eyes swung around the room and came to rest on Felicia. "You look magnificent," he said.

He had overlooked the bleak expression in her eyes. All he could see was the dazzle of her expensive clothes, the professional hairstyle and makeup.

"Thanks," Felicia said, hoping to divert Don's attention from the expensive surroundings. "Won't you have a seat?" she offered awkwardly.

It was only now that she realized how she had avoided Don. She had promised to call him, but so much had been happening lately, she had hardly given him a second thought.

Don sat down on the velvet couch, and Felicia took a place on the other end. "You said you'd call," Don explained his dropping by unannounced. "When I didn't hear from you, I thought maybe something had happened. I got your forwarding address. I came by to see how you are."

"I'm just fine, Don," Felicia said.

"So I see." There was a strained silence. "How is your mother?"

"Oh, much better," Felicia said with a faint smile. "She finally agreed to see me. We're on good terms now. I even took her out for her birthday last night. She got a pass from the hospital."

"I see," Don said woodenly. His tone said he knew it was all over between them. "Well, I guess there's nothing more to say."

"What do you mean?"

"It's pretty obvious. You didn't call. You're set up here in a fine apartment. Your whole life has changed . . . and I don't fit in it anymore."

"That's not true, Don," Felicia protested, anxiety nibbling at her. "I've just been so busy."

"Like tonight?" Don asked. "Were you too busy to call tonight?"

The obvious reference to her free time this evening, during which she could have called Don, made her uncomfortable.

"W-well . . ." she stammered.

"Felicia, you've changed so much. You don't look the same. There's a whole different aura surrounding you now. You look very settled in here, in all this," he said, his arm sweeping the air, indicating the posh interior of her apartment.

"It's temporary, Don," Felicia pointed out. "It's part of my job. But my contract is only for a year. Then I'll move back to my old apartment, get my job back at the high school."

"You'll never come back, Felicia," Don said.

"Of course I will," Felicia protested. "I'm doing this for my mother. The rich life isn't for me. All I want to do is settle down someday and have a family. I want to raise a couple of kids. I'm just an ordinary girl with ordinary ambitions."

"That's how you started out," Don said softly. "But

there's something about you now, something much different. It's hard to define. But it's there."

"What are you talking about?"

"It's a kind of determination you didn't have before. You're a different person now, Felicia. You didn't intend to let it happen to you, but you've lost that hometown-girl quality you once had. You're more sophisticated."

"Oh, Don, don't be silly." Felicia laughed nervously. "It's just my clothes and this apartment. I haven't changed."

"Yes, you have, Felicia," Don corrected her. "In a very subtle but basic way."

Just then the phone rang. Felicia considered letting it ring without answering it, but she found herself rising from the sofa in response to its demand.

"Hello," she said.

"Miss Farr," came the polished female voice on the other end. "Mr. Bearstern has set up another shooting session, on location this time."

"Oh?"

"Yes, he wants you to be ready to fly out at 6:30 in the morning."

"All right," Felicia agreed. "Where's it to be?"

"In San Francisco."

"That should be interesting," Felicia commented. "I've never been there."

She ended the conversation and joined Don on the sofa again. Don looked at her quizzically.

"I have to fly to San Francisco tomorrow for some location shooting," she answered his silent question.

"You really are enjoying yourself, aren't you?" Don said. "I guess I can't blame you."

"Of course not," Felicia protested. "I told you, I'm doing this for my mother. It's temporary. It means less than nothing to me."

"If you could have heard yourself on the phone, you

would agree that I'm right. Your tone of voice . . . it said it all."

"Don, there's no point in my running around angry all the time, now is there?" Felicia pointed out weakly. Her own argument was beginning to sound a little hollow. "I'm stuck with this for a year, so I might as well make the best of a bad situation."

"Sure," Don said in a tone that revealed he wasn't convinced. "Well, I better be going. You need your rest to look your best for the cameras tomorrow."

"But it's early," Felicia said, with a little pout.

"No, Felicia," Don said somberly. "It's late, too late. Good night."

And then she was alone with her thoughts. Was there truth in Don's observations? Had she succumbed to the allure of this glamorous, affluent life? Had she changed without realizing it? The answer came to her quite clearly. Yes, she had changed, but not because of her surroundings or her modeling career. She had changed because she had found her own identity. She was her own person now, secure in the knowledge, and suddenly more adult and sure of herself than ever before in her life. Don had thought her more "determined," more "sophisticated." He had not understood the real change that had taken place in her.

She was sad to see Don go, for she had been genuinely fond of him. But it was best for both of them. Don had spoken the truth when he had said, "It's late, too late." Yes, it was too late for them.

Suddenly the phone rang, breaking into her reverie.

It was Dr. Ambrewster. "Felicia, your mother has had a heart attack. Could you come to the hospital tonight? I need to talk to you."

Chapter Nine

"An operation?" Felicia choked, tears stinging her eyes.

She was seated before Dr. Ambrewster's desk in a small office room in the hospital. "I'm afraid so," he replied, his face serious. "I thought I should be the one to tell you. Your mother has been making fine progress with her emotional problems. I think a good deal of the credit goes to you. But she has physical problems too. I've been treating her for a heart condition for some time. Her heart has been deteriorating lately. She didn't want you to know about it. She didn't want to spoil the joy both of you have been having at finding each other again. I suppose she's been trying to hide her condition from herself. But she had a heart attack this afternoon. We can't bury our heads in the sand about this situation any longer. Your mother simply has to have open heart surgery. She cannot put it off any longer."

"She . . . she must have had a pretty bad attack to make the surgery so urgent. . . ."

"Well, it was a warning attack. But a pretty darn good indication of what we're in for if we don't take steps right now to correct her problem. Another attack could be fatal."

"Fatal?" Felicia gasped.

"Yes," Dr. Ambrewster nodded soberly. "I don't want to frighten you, Felicia. But I think it's important that you understand the situation. I called you here to explain fully what she's up against. She needs that operation. It's delicate and it's costly. You've already had a mountain of expenses, coping with her psychiatric care. Would you be able to cope with this additional expense of an operation?"

"You mean if I can't pay for the operation, you'd just let her die?" Felicia demanded.

"Certainly not. Don't think that for a moment. We have some pretty good local surgeons. If necessary, she could become a charity case and the county would see that she had as good care as could be provided locally. But I'd really like to call in a specialist in this field. Now *that* gets expensive. As you know, your mother has no insurance at all, and—"

"A specialist? Who would you recommend?"

"I'd like to bring in Dr. Landrum from Chicago. He has an international reputation with this particular kind of surgery."

"Would he come . . . if I can pay his fee?"

"Yes. I've already talked to him by phone. His fee plus the hospital costs will be staggering, but . . ."

Dr. Ambrewster quoted an estimated cost that made Felicia's head swim. But she took a deep breath and settled herself against her own emotions. There was one way to come up with that kind of money fast, and she knew how to do it. The price she would have to pay was enormous, not in dollars and cents alone, but she was prepared to do anything to provide the very best medical care for her mother.

"All right," Felicia said. "Call Dr. Landrum. Make arrangements. I can get the money."

Dr. Ambrewster smiled with relief. "I knew I could count on you."

"Yeah," Felicia responded with dismal resignation. She left Dr. Ambrewster's office with a heavy heart. She took a cab directly to Roderick's office, knowing that if she delayed, she might weaken and change her mind.

The secretary buzzed Roderick as soon as Felicia asked to see him.

"He's on a long-distance call," she explained, "but he'll see you as soon as he's finished."

"Thanks," Felicia said woodenly. She sat in the outer office for what seemd like forever, but in fact, it was only a few minutes before Roderick appeared in the doorway to his office and motioned for her to come in.

Felicia heaved a deep sigh. What choice did she have, she asked herself? True, she was making enough money to pay for her mother's psychiatric care, but this operation was something else again. She would need a big slug of money in one pop, and there was only one way she could get it.

"Well, hello," Roderick said warmly. "This is a pleasant surprise. Sit down."

Felicia took the familiar overstuffed chair she had sat in so many times before. Roderick perched in his usual pose on the front edge of his desk, towering over her, demolishing her defenses against him by his nearness. What she had come to say was hard enough without having to fight the pounding of her heart and the rush of warm blood to her cheeks when Roderick bent over and looked at her expectantly. All she could see for a moment was the dark hair against the olive complexion, the green flecks dancing in his brown eyes, the square jaw that she longed to trail her fingers over. Why did he affect her this way, she demanded silently of herself.

"Is this a business call or a personal one?" Roderick asked, his eyes slowly sliding down her frame and pausing appreciatively on the swell of her breasts straining at the lightweight silk blouse with a V neckline.

"Strictly business," she replied haughtily.

"Too bad," Roderick mused.

She ignored his suggestive comment. "You still want to promote me as the Magic Glo Girl, don't you?" she asked.

"Of course. The campaign is already under way."

"And what would you say if I agreed to work for you longer than just a year?"

"I'd say you've come to your senses," Roderick smiled.

"Well," she hedged. "I might be persuaded to sign another contract with you." She paused, her large blue eyes swinging up to meet Roderick's penetrating brown ones.

"And just what would it take to persuade you?"

Felicia looked down at her lap in embarrassment. She picked the cuticle of one hand. She knew that when she told Roderick what she wanted, he was going to jump to the wrong conclusion. But she wasn't about to tell him the truth. It was none of his business. He knew far too much about her already. And it was unlikely he still had his detectives snooping around since he had her wrapped up with a neat little contract.

She hated for him to think she had succumbed to the rich life, but if he knew the truth, he would devise some way to use it against her. So, he'd just have to think the worst. Maybe it was even better that way.

"I want a sizable advance."

"Of course," Roderick agreed easily. "So you've found you can't live on your current salary? I knew it wouldn't take you long."

Felicia's cheeks burned angrily. "I haven't told you how much I want yet," she said stonily.

"Okay, how much?" Roderick asked.

Felicia quoted a figure she felt sure would make Roderick balk, but he merely smiled.

"Are you sure that's enough?" he asked.

"Quite enough," Felicia said flatly. "In spite of what you may think, I don't plan to stay indebted to you forever."

"Of course not," Roderick said, his voice clearly indicating he thought he had Felicia hooked for good.

"I want the money right away," Felicia said.

"All right. I'll have my lawyer draw up your contract, you sign it, and I can have a check in your hands in a few days."

"That's not good enough," Felicia protested. "I want the money right away—tomorrow."

"That's not possible." Roderick laughed as if dealing with an impatient child.

"Tomorrow or not at all," Felicia issued an ultimatum.

"Why so desperate?" Roderick asked suspiciously.

"Because I might change my mind," Felicia said, her answer calculated to force Roderick into submission.

"All right," Roderick agreed. "I'll have the lawyer draw up the contract immediately. I'll give you my personal check for the advance as soon as you've signed. Then I'll collect the advance from the bookkeeping department when the check is issued. Is that satisfactory?"

"Quite," she said, holding her tumultuous emotions in check. She hated what she was doing, but she knew no other way. How could she bear being around

Roderick for heaven knew how long? She had to make it clear how long this new contract would last.

"As to the time element, I think an additional year as the Magic Glo Girl should satisfy you for the amount you're advancing me."

"Yes, I think so," Roderick smiled. "But then, what are you going to live on once you've spent the advance? Or are you investing it?"

"One year, Roderick," Felicia said determinedly. "And *I'll* worry about my finances."

"Sure," Roderick said with a deep chuckle, which indicated he saw this as just the first of a long line of one year contracts Felicia would be signing with him in the future. "Whatever your reasons, Felicia, you've made the right decision. You're going to be a superstar model. You don't have to give up your whole life the way your mother did. The longer you're in this business, the better you're going to like it. It gets in your blood after a while."

"Yeah," Felicia muttered glumly. She had already seen just how quickly this business had gotten into her blood. But it wasn't because she was crazy about the work. It was because she was desperate for the big money. No matter how good her motivation, she realized she had sold herself twice for money, and she felt the need to go home and take a long, hot bath to wash away the dirty aspects of this business.

Felicia left Roderick's office in a dark mood. She was jubilant over being able to help her mother, but nothing could vanquish the dismal cloud that engulfed her with its chilly atmosphere. It wasn't the modeling so much, really, she realized. It was having Roderick Bearstern thinking he had won. And it was knowing the heartache she was letting herself in for, having to be around a man she loved and hated, a man who cared absolutely nothing for her as a person.

Once back in her apartment, Felicia picked up the

phone and dialed a number she knew all too well, but which she had avoided calling of late.

Don answered.

"Hi," Felicia said, trying to infuse her voice with a touch of warmth she no longer felt.

"Hello," Don said without emotion. Felicia knew he recognized her voice.

"This is Felicia," she said as lightly as she could.

"I know," Don replied. "How are you?"

"Just fine," Felicia lied, refusing to reveal the bargain she had just struck with Roderick, refusing to let the bitterness over the rocky road her life had taken seep into her voice.

"Don," Felicia grew serious. "I just thought I should let you know. My mother's had a heart attack. She's going to have to have open heart surgery."

"Oh, Felicia, I'm very sorry," Don commented sincerely, but it was a tone of impersonal concern, such as a newspaper reader might express for a stranger whose misfortune he had read about in the paper. "Is there anything I can do?"

Is there anything I can do? Felicia repeated mentally. Those were the noncommittal words we all used when we offered to help someone whom we expected would not take us up on the offer. Don didn't ask, Can I come over and sit with you during the operation? He didn't say he would come right over and stay with her through her wait for the operation to begin. He didn't offer anything specific. Merely the question, Is there anything I can do?

"No," Felicia said sadly. "I—I just thought you should know."

"I hope she pulls through all right," Don commented before Felicia ended the conversation.

"Thanks," was her final reply.

Well, what had she expected, she asked herself. She had known in her heart that things were truly over between her and Don. But she hadn't wanted to accept that fact. If she could have held on to the illusion that they still meant something to each other, she could have refused to believe another fact: Her life had changed permanently.

She could never return to teaching. Soon her picture would be plastered all over America, maybe the world. Once that happened, once she became the famed Magic Glo Girl, she could never go back to the classroom. Her effectiveness as a teacher would be destroyed. The boys would all ogle her, and the girls would try to compete with her. How could she keep their minds on the subject matter under those circumstances?

That night Felicia cried herself to sleep. She cried for her lost destiny, she cried for her mother and the unhappy life she had led, she cried for her relationship with Don now turned to ashes. But most of all she cried from heartache over the one man she would love the rest of her life but could never have, Roderick Bearstern.

Two mornings later, Felicia sat outside the hospital waiting room. She stared silently at the light green wall opposite her.

She had actually done it. She had committed herself to Roderick for another year, had collected her advance and had told Dr. Ambrewster to go ahead with her mother's operation. The speed with which final arrangements were concluded boggled her mind. She had met with Dr. Landrum briefly and had seen her mother only a few moments before the attendants wheeled Francine into the operating room.

And now she sat alone. What an ironic twist, Felicia thought sadly. Her mother had once been the toast of the continent, and now she had only one lone visitor to worry about her through a delicate, dangerous operation. Where were all Francine's admirers now? Regardless of what happened to her, of how popular she became, Felicia would never forget this moment. The adoration of fickle fans meant absolutely nothing in the long run, she realized. What truly mattered were the enduring relationships of family and genuine friends.

In spite of what Francine had done to Felicia, it was she, Francine's daughter, a blood relative, who had helped her mother and who was willing to sacrifice for her well-being.

Suddenly Felicia's ruminations were interrupted by the vision of a tall, dark man striding down the hallway toward her. Her pulse quickened, her mouth became dry. What was Roderick doing here?

As soon as he strode within earshot, Felicia could no longer remain silent. "What are you doing here?" she asked hoarsely.

"Have you heard anything about your mother, yet?" Roderick asked, stopping in front of her, taking her hands in his.

Felicia's heart stopped, and a phantom hand squeezed her chest until she was breathless. Roderick's hands were large, warm and comforting. Her hands were cold and shaking.

"How did you know about my mother?" Felicia asked.

"My usual sources," Roderick said casually. "You seemed so determined to have that money, Felicia. I knew you hadn't run up a bunch of frivolous bills. You're too level-headed for that. But when I baited you, you didn't deny my accusations. So I had my sources check to find out if you were in some kind of trouble."

"Roderick Bearstern!" Felicia snapped, jerking her

hands back from his. "How dare you spy on me again! I have a right to my privacy. I want you to keep out of my private life, do you hear?"

"Felicia, I know you're upset . . ." Roderick began in a soothing voice.

"You're darn right I'm upset!" Felicia exploded. "This is a private matter, and you have no right to intrude. What's the matter, were you afraid your precious Magic Glo Girl might have done something to tarnish her reputation?"

"Not at all."

"Well, I don't believe you," Felicia said icily. "You're not concerned about me as a person. You're a plastic person who doesn't give a darn about the real needs and concerns of others. You just want to protect your investment. You had your little spies out checking up on me to make sure your newest model didn't do anything to make the front page unless you orchestrated it."

"If that were true, why did I bother to come here today?" Roderick asked pointedly. "Once I had the information I needed, I knew there was nothing I could do except offer moral support. That's why I'm here."

Before Felicia could digest the impact of Roderick's words, the double doors leading into the operating room a few feet down the hall swung open. Dr. Ambrewster came out, his head covered with a green surgical cap, his face party hidden behind a matching surgical mask, and his body camouflaged by a green gown.

"She's all prepped," Dr. Ambrewster said as soon as Felicia had hurried to his side. "Dr. Landrum will start the operation in a few minutes. I'll send someone out periodically to let you know how she's progressing."

"Thank you," Felicia said gratefully. "Do you . . . do you—"

"Yes, Felicia," Dr. Ambrewster reassured her. "I

think she's going to make it just fine. As I said, Dr. Landrum is the best. Now, I promised your mother I'd stay right by her side for the entire operation, so I'd better get back in there."

"Oh, Dr. Ambrewster, thank you," Felicia said, her voice shaking with emotion. At that moment, she wanted to throw her arms around the doctor and give him a big hug, but the surgical green meant she should not contaminate him.

Felicia returned to her chair in the waiting room. Roderick was standing, silently waiting for her.

"It's starting now," she informed him, momentarily forgetting her anger. She sat down, and Roderick followed suit. She was grateful he hadn't left. Right now, she didn't want to be alone, even if she had to share this time with Roderick Bearstern.

"I'll stay as long as you need me," Roderick said softly.

"Thanks," Felicia said, and a strange warmth ran through her. For that moment, Roderick seemed truly human, like a man with the heart and soul of a caring person. He had offered to stay as long as she needed him. What a strange twist of fate, she thought. Up until now, it was Roderick who had needed her—needed her to carry out his Francine Farr revival. She had never thought she would someday need him. She loved him and she wanted him, but needing him—that was a new experience for her. And right now she needed him very much.

Felicia looked at Roderick and caught him eyeing her with a curious expression on his face. He looked at her silently, and for a long moment, their eyes met and embraced each other in a long-distance encounter of two souls meeting on the brink of an uncharted sea where ships often collided in the murky waters.

What did it mean? Felicia asked herself when she finally tore her eyes from Roderick's stare. She didn't know the answer to that question, but her beating heart and shaking hands told her it had been more than an expression of sympathy for her plight.

Felicia and Roderick sat in silence as the time ticked by slowly on the large wall clock across from them. Occasionally, a nurse came to the double doors, poked her head out and announced that Francine was just fine and that the operation was proceeding as scheduled.

Felicia paced the floor for a while, holding her hands pressed tightly against her stomach. She sat down again for a while. She looked up once to see Roderick holding out a cup of coffee to her. She smiled weakly, took the cup and mumbled "Thank you."

The waiting, the waiting. It was almost unbearable. But Roderick's presence made the situation tolerable. If only Felicia could have told him so, if only she could have said how much she loved him. But she was certain he was not here because of any personal concern for her. He was merely looking out for his financial interest in his Magic Glo Girl. If her mother did not survive the operation, he wanted to be nearby to see she was taken care of. He didn't want her sinking into a depression that would make her unable to work.

Finally, Dr. Ambrewster and Dr. Landrum pushed through the double doors together, pulling the surgical masks from their faces.

"She's fine, Felicia," Dr. Ambrewster reassured her, squeezing her hands in his.

"Yes," Dr. Landrum agreed. "Basically, she's a very strong woman. I expect a complete recovery. Of course, she'll have to take it easy for a while."

Tears of relief filled Felicia's eyes. "Oh, Dr. Ambrewster, Dr. Landrum, thank you," she gushed. "Thank you."

"We're just as overjoyed as you are," Dr. Landrum said.

"Yes, I can tell you are," Felicia said happily. It was obvious both doctors cared a great deal for their patients. It was a quality money couldn't buy in a doctor.

As soon as the doctors had left, Roderick stood up to go. "I want to see you in my office as soon as possible," Roderick said.

"Of course," Felicia replied frostily. So already Roderick's mind had returned to business, Felicia thought bitterly. Here were two doctors who cared almost as much about their patients as if they were relatives. And then there was Roderick Bearstern, who probably would sell his mother down the river if it suited his purposes. How could she have fallen in love with such a heartless man? She hated him for his ruthlessness, but there was a part of her heart that would love him forever, no matter how loathesome he might be.

After Roderick had left, Felicia waited the rest of the afternoon while her mother was monitored closely in the recovery room. Later that evening, Francine was wheeled back into her own room. Felicia was waiting for her.

"She'll be heavily sedated for the next couple of days," the nurse explained. "To control the pain."

Felicia spent the next forty-eight hours at the hospital, dozing in the chair, pacing the floor to pass the time, trying to read magazines.

On the morning of the third day, Felicia was looking out of the hospital window at the parking lot below, when she heard a whisper behind her.

"Mother?" she called softly, turning to face the bed.

"Is that you, Felicia?" responded a weak, shy voice.

"Yes, Mother, I'm here," Felicia reassured her.

"What day is it?" Francine asked groggily.

"Wednesday."

177

"I guess I'm not thinking straight," her mother said in a befuddled voice. "I thought they'd just wheeled me into the operating room. . . ."

"You've been under sedation," Felicia told her, giving her hand a warm squeeze. "But everything's going to be just fine, Mother. The operation was a complete success. You're going to be well very soon."

A nurse entered the room and gave Francine an injection. Soon she drifted back to sleep. Felicia quietly left the room.

But she didn't go home. A nurse gave her a message. Roderick's office had telephoned, reminding her that he wanted her to report to his office. Felicia was furious. He was so callous, he wanted her to go back to work immediately! The man had no heart whatsoever. He was only interested in the money she could earn for his company! His main worry was that she would lose time from work.

She took a cab to Roderick's office.

She marched into his office and past his secretary without so much as a word. She flung open the door to his inner office and strode in unannounced.

Roderick was sitting behind his desk, hunched over a stack of papers, writing something. At the sound of the door opening, he looked up. His brown eyes sparkled with green.

"Felicia," he exclaimed. "I didn't expect you so soon."

"I bet you didn't!" she fumed.

Roderick stood up. "Sit down," he ordered solemnly. "I have something to give you."

"I don't want anything from you!" she said coldly.

"This, you do," he said in a mysterious, knowing tone that took Felicia off guard.

She opened her mouth to give him a piece of her mind, but she stopped as he reached down, picked up the paper he had been writing on and shoved it in her hands.

"Here," he said tightly. "Look at this."

"What is it?" she asked suspiciously.

"Look at it," he commanded.

Tentatively, Felicia let her eyes trail down to her hands. It was a legal-looking document, which she recognized as a contract with Roderick's company.

"So?" she demanded.

"Look closer," he instructed her.

"Is this some kind of game?" Felicia asked hostilely.

"Do as I tell you!" Roderick said with exasperation. He lifted her hands so the contract was inches from her eyes. Then he turned his back on her and stood with his weight resting on his hands spread out on his desk, his shoulders hunched over.

Felicia stood looking at Roderick's strong, muscular back straining at the fabric of his dark coat. For a moment, she felt the urge to run to him, put her arms around him and ask him what was wrong. The bitter anger of a few minutes ago was lost in the stance of dismay Roderick had assumed at his desk.

Then she turned her attention to the sheath of papers in her hand. It was a modeling contract with her name on it, and across the front had been written in large red letters, the word "Cancelled." Under the bold word which voided the agreement, Roderick Bearstern had signed his name, with today's date. There was a second contract, her most recent one, with the same red inscription.

"I—I don't understand," Felicia mumbled, unbelieving.

Roderick did not turn to face her. "I'm no longer going to hold you to your contract," he said simply, his voice deep and thick.

"But why?" Felicia asked incredulously.

"I have my reasons," Roderick said, turning to face her, his eyes strangely clouded, his mouth grim.

For a moment, Felicia felt a burst of joy at being released from the bondage she had felt at Roderick's hands. But immediately, she felt something else she couldn't at first define. Then, gradually, she realized what the aching in her chest was all about. As long as she was under contract to Roderick, she would have to continue seeing him, no matter how painful those encounters might be for her. But this way, with her contracts cancelled, she would no longer have any excuse for seeing Roderick, and she realized for the first time that not seeing him at all was far worse than the heartache she experienced in his presence.

"You don't have to do that," she protested. "I knew what I was doing when I signed those contracts. I fully intended to honor them."

"But you signed them under duress," Roderick pointed out. "If it hadn't been for your mother's need for hospital care, you would never have agreed to work for me. I've decided I can't hold you to your contract under the circumstances."

Felicia stood dumbfounded. She had never expected Roderick to feel enough compassion for another human being to set aside his own interests for someone else's sake. Could he actually harbor inside that hard exterior a little touch of humanity? Or did he have some ulterior motive she didn't know about yet?

Maybe it was simply that she had made herself so unbearable around him that he didn't want to be bothered with her anymore. If that was the case, he certainly was willing to pay a high price to get rid of her.

"All right," Felicia agreed. "I'm glad you're canceling my contracts. But let me assure you, Mr. Bearstern," she said caustically, "that I intend to pay back every penny you've advanced me. I don't know how long it will take, but you can rest assured I'll satisfy my debt to you, with interest, even if it takes forever."

With that, Felicia threw the contracts on Roderick's desk and rushed from his office, tears streaming down her cheeks.

Chapter Ten

"Oh, Mother, I've been such a fool," Felicia exclaimed, trying to hold back her tears.

The hospital room, with its bright yellow interior, was in direct contrast to the cloud of sadness hanging over Felicia.

"I should be so thankful that you're all right and well on the road to recovery," Felicia admitted, "that what happened between Roderick and me doesn't matter all that much."

"Of course it matters," Francine said softly. She was propped up in the hopsital bed. Her eyes were bright, her color much improved since the operation. She said softly, "Why don't you go to Roderick and tell him how you feel?"

"I couldn't do that," Felicia replied, shaking her head. "I'd be making a silly fool out of myself. Roderick doesn't care for me. I was just an advertising campaign to him."

"Are you really sure? I'd hate for you to spend your life in love with a man without his even knowing it, the way my situation has been with Roderick's father."

Felicia squeezed her mother's hand with a sudden rush of heartache for her. "I'm so sorry, Mother. I wish I could make things better for you—make up for all the disappointments you've had."

"But you already have," Francine said warmly. "Forgiving me the way you did, loving me and letting us become friends these past weeks—it more than made up for the bad things that happened to me. But you're still young enough to alter the course of your life. I really think you should swallow your pride and tell Roderick Bearstern how you feel about him. Make certain he doesn't return your love before you give up. Perhaps he's a captive of his pride, too."

Felicia shook her head again. "It would be useless, Mother," she said grimly. "I know all too well how Roderick feels about me. He's made it quite clear."

Then, despite her mother's protest, Felicia changed the subject. They talked about future plans, about the time when Francine would be strong enough to leave the hospital. Felicia planned to rent a larger apartment for the both of them. "I still have my teaching certificate," she said optimistically. "And there's always a job for a teacher somewhere—"

She was interrupted by the hospital door opening. She turned and saw two men entering the room. Both had square jawlines, dark eyes, jet black hair and olive skin that reflected Indian blood. The younger of the two, Roderick Bearstern, of course. And the older man . . . Felicia saw a definite resemblance between the two men. She heard her mother utter a soft exclamation, and she knew it must be Roderick's father, John Bearstern!

She was momentarily struck speechless with surprise. She glanced at her mother. Francine's face was flushed and animated. Felicia thought, Why she's never looked more beautiful!

Dimly, she heard her mother say, "John! This is quite a surprise."

Felicia was vaguely aware of Roderick's voice.

"Felicia, I'd like you to meet my father. Dad, this is Francine's daughter, Felicia."

"How do you do, young lady. I've heard a lot about you, and all of it is true. You certainly inherited your mother's beauty."

Felicia stammered some kind of reply. She was unable to tear her surprised gaze from Roderick's face.

Roderick was speaking to her mother, then. "You probably don't remember me, Mrs. Farr. I was just starting in the business during the last months of your modeling career. But I've been an admirer of yours all my life."

"Thank you," Francine said softly. And her eyes swung back toward Roderick's father.

"I'd heard you were ill, Francine," John Bearstern said. He had moved to a position beside the bed and had taken Francine's hand, holding it between his large fingers. "I tried to visit you before, but the doctors told me you were not accepting visitors."

"I'm glad you came, John," Francine replied. "I'm much better now. Much better in every way."

Felicia was aware that Roderick had moved to her side. She felt his strong hand take possession of her arm. "Why don't we go downstairs for a cup of coffee and let the older generation visit."

His father scowled at him. " 'Older' generation! You young whippersnapper. Meet me on the golf course tomorrow morning, and I'll show you which one of us is in better shape."

"No way." Roderick chuckled. "I remember the trouncing you gave me the last time. Come on, Felicia."

Still in a daze, she allowed him to steer her out of the room. She glanced back once before the door closed and saw John Bearstern still holding Francine's hand, speaking to her in a low, intimate voice.

"You have a good relationship with your father, don't you?" Felicia said as Roderick led her to the elevator.

"Yes, I'm glad to say we're very close. I admire him, and he respects me. We're good friends until we get on the golf course. Then"—Roderick chuckled—"I become his mortal enemy."

"I'm so happy he wanted to come see my mother. It means a lot to her."

"It means a lot to him. He's been very upset since I told him about Francine's surgery. He really did try to get in to see her several times the past months, but she wasn't seeing anybody."

Felicia looked up at Roderick. "I don't know if I should tell you this, but your father is very special to my mother—more than just an acquaintance."

"I'm glad to hear that. I'd hate to have a broken-hearted senior citizen on my hands. You know, in spite of the grief Dad put up with coping with my mother's alcoholism, he was faithful to her until she died. But I always suspected if he hadn't been married, and your mother hadn't been married, he and Francine might have made a couple. Several comments he's made in the past gave me a clue that he had a crush on your mother, but he kept it to himself."

Tears of joy suddenly blinded her. That was the best news she'd had in a long time. How wonderful, she thought, if at last the tragedy that had haunted her mother all her life would end in happiness for her.

"Here's the elevator," she heard Roderick say.

"Listen," she told him, "you don't have to feel obligated to buy me a cup of coffee. I realize you just came here to bring your father to see my mother. You go on to the coffee shop. I'll just wait over there in the lounge area. . . ."

Roderick scowled fiercely at her. "You're not going to brush me off so easily this time. Get in there!"

He practically shoved her into the elevator.

The doors closed and the elevator began to descend. Then Roderick pressed a red button, stopping the car between floors.

"What are you doing?" Felicia gasped.

"I'm making sure you don't get away from me the way your mother got away from my father for so many years."

"What?"

"Let's forget about your mother and my father for a minute," Roderick continued, "and concentrate on us."

"On us?" Felicia choked.

"Yes," Roderick said, his dark eyes becoming swirling black pools. Then he said, "I know how you feel about me. . . ."

She felt her heart pound, her cheeks flush. "You . . . do?"

"Yes, I know you hate me and think me a ruthless scoundrel. You've made it clear you want to have nothing to do with me."

"W-well—" she stammered.

"But in spite of that," he interrupted, "I'm not going to make the same kind of mistake my father did, Felicia. I love you. I want to marry you. And I'm not going to take no for an answer. I almost let you slip away from me when I cancelled your contract. I realized I could no longer bind you to me against your will. But after you were gone, I felt miserable. I didn't know when I would see you again, if ever. I took stock of my self, my life, and I realized what a complete fool I've been. I was attracted to you from the start, and I realized that somewhere along the way I had fallen in love with you. When was it? I think it was that day you waltzed into the studio with your hair and makeup changed so you looked like yourself instead of a carbon copy of Francine and defied me to do anything about it. I wasn't fully aware of it at the time, but now I know my feeling for you underwent a big change from that moment on."

He was holding her hands tightly, capturing her gaze with the hypnotic intensity of his eyes. "I thought about it a lot, and I realize that it had been my memory of your glamorous mother that kept me from seeing you as a real person. I had such an obsession about her, ever since I was a young man, that I could only think of re-creating her. I was in love with the past, with a glamorous illusion. Then you jolted me to reality when you asserted your independence—when you found your own identity and forced me to see you as Felicia, not the ghost of Francine. And it's Felicia I love and want. I'm not going to give you up. I want you for my wife, and I mean to have you. And you should know by now that when I want something, I get it. Whether you like it or not, Felicia Farr, I'm going to make you learn to love me!"

"You are?" she asked in a small voice.

"Of course I am," he said determinedly. "I may have picked a bad way to deal with you in the past, because I thought you hated me. But I'm telling you up front I love you this time, and I'm not letting you get away from me again."

"You aren't?" Felicia gazed at him, a tremulous joy singing in her heart.

"Well," he demanded, "what do you say to that?"

"I'm not sure." She shrugged, hiding a sudden flash of mischievous happiness in her eyes.

He seized her and kissed her passionately. *"Now* what do you say to that?" he asked.

"I don't know," she murmured dreamily. "Try it again. . . ."

IT'S YOUR OWN SPECIAL TIME

Contemporary romances for today's women.
Each month, six very special love stories will be yours
from SILHOUETTE. Look for them wherever books are sold
or order now from the coupon below.

$1.50 each

Hampson	☐ 1 ☐ 4 ☐ 16 ☐ 27 ☐ 28 ☐ 40 ☐ 52 ☐ 64 ☐ 94	Browning	☐ 12 ☐ 38 ☐ 53 ☐ 73 ☐ 93
Stanford	☐ 6 ☐ 25 ☐ 35 ☐ 46 ☐ 58 ☐ 88	Michaels	☐ 15 ☐ 32 ☐ 61 ☐ 87
		John	☐ 17 ☐ 34 ☐ 57 ☐ 85
Hastings	☐ 13 ☐ 26 ☐ 44 ☐ 67	Beckman	☐ 8 ☐ 37 ☐ 54 ☐ 72 ☐ 96
Vitek	☐ 33 ☐ 47 ☐ 66 ☐ 84		

$1.50 each

☐ 3 Powers	☐ 29 Wildman	☐ 56 Trent	☐ 79 Halldorson
☐ 5 Goforth	☐ 30 Dixon	☐ 59 Vernon	☐ 80 Stephens
☐ 7 Lewis	☐ 31 Halldorson	☐ 60 Hill	☐ 81 Roberts
☐ 9 Wilson	☐ 36 McKay	☐ 62 Hallston	☐ 82 Dailey
☐ 10 Caine	☐ 39 Sinclair	☐ 63 Brent	☐ 83 Hallston
☐ 11 Vernon	☐ 41 Owen	☐ 69 St. George	☐ 86 Adams
☐ 14 Oliver	☐ 42 Powers	☐ 70 Afton Bonds	☐ 89 James
☐ 19 Thornton	☐ 43 Robb	☐ 71 Ripy	☐ 90 Major
☐ 20 Fulford	☐ 45 Carroll	☐ 74 Trent	☐ 92 McKay
☐ 21 Richards	☐ 48 Wildman	☐ 75 Carroll	☐ 95 Wisdom
☐ 22 Stephens	☐ 49 Wisdom	☐ 76 Hardy	☐ 97 Clay
☐ 23 Edwards	☐ 50 Scott	☐ 77 Cork	☐ 98 St. George
☐ 24 Healy	☐ 55 Ladame	☐ 78 Oliver	☐ 99 Camp

$1.75 each

☐ 100 Stanford	☐ 104 Vitek	☐ 108 Hampson	☐ 112 Stanford
☐ 101 Hardy	☐ 105 Eden	☐ 109 Vernon	☐ 113 Browning
☐ 102 Hastings	☐ 106 Dailey	☐ 110 Trent	☐ 114 Michaels
☐ 103 Cork	☐ 107 Bright	☐ 111 South	☐ 115 John
	☐ 116 Lindley	☐ 117 Scott	

Introducing
First Love from
Silhouette Romances for
teenage girls
to build their dreams on.

They're wholesome, fulfilling, supportive novels about every
young girl's dreams. Filled with the challenges, excitement—
and responsibilities—of love's first blush, *First Love* paper-
backs prepare young adults to stand at the threshold of
maturity with confidence and composure.

Introduce your daughter, or some young friend to the
First Love series by giving her a one-year subscription to
these romantic originals, written by leading authors. She'll
receive two NEW $1.75 romances each month, a total of 24
books a year. Send in your coupon now. **There's nothing
quite as special as a First Love.**

Silhouette **Romance**

15-Day Free Trial Offer
6 Silhouette Romances

6 Silhouette Romances, free for 15 days! We'll send you 6 new Silhouette Romances to keep for 15 days, absolutely free! If you decide not to keep them, send them back to us. You pay nothing.

Free Home Delivery. But if you enjoy them as much as we think you will, keep them by paying the invoice enclosed with your free trial shipment. We'll pay all shipping and handling charges. You get the convenience of Home Delivery and we pay the postage and handling charge each month.

Don't miss a copy. The Silhouette Book Club is the way to make sure you'll be able to receive every new romance we publish before they're sold out. There is no minimum number of books to buy and you can cancel at any time.

This offer expires June 30, 1982

Silhouette Book Club, Dept. SBK 17B
120 Brighton Road, Clifton, NJ 07012

Please send me 6 Silhouette Romances to keep for 15 days, absolutely free. I understand I am not obligated to join the Silhouette Book Club unless I decide to keep them.

NAME_____

ADDRESS_____

CITY_____ STATE_____ZIP_____